Wild n Free

A collection of winning wild animal
stories by children

For Elsa the Lioness, where it all started

PAWS N CLAWS PUBLISHING

Paws n Claws Publishing, Clwt Y Bont, Wales

www.pawsnclawspublishing.co.uk

This book copyright ©Paws n Claws Publishing 2012
First edition published 2012 by Paws n Claws Publishing

All rights reserved
Edited by Debz Hobbs-Wyatt
Designed and Typeset by *www.lksdesigns.co.uk*

British Library Cataloguing in Publication Data
A Record of this Publication is available from the British Library

ISBN 978-0-9568939-4-9

All Paws n Claws books are published on paper derived from
sustainable resources

Acknowledgements

A lot of people are involved in putting a project like this together, from the schools, and the charity who helped promote the competition through to our lovely graphic designer, Lisa Simmonds, for putting it together into the lovely book you hold in your hands.

I really need to give special mention to my preliminary team of fabulously talented writers/readers who helped to select the shortlist, Anita, Carol, Dorothy, Dulcie, Gill, Holly, Julie-Ann, Kirsty, Pat, Pauline and Shan. And then to our prestigious judges Alan Gibbons, Lauren St.John and Virginia McKenna for making the final selection.

I also want to thank Colin and Justin Wyatt, our professional artists, for helping to select the drawings.

Thanks to Born Free for their support throughout and to all of the children and their families for helping me bring it all together.

Debz

Born Free is a dynamic international wildlife charity, devoted to compassionate conservation and animal welfare. Born Free believes wildlife belongs in the wild and works to phase out zoos and stop animal exploitation. Born Free rescues individuals and gives them lifetime care. With local communities, Born Free protects lions, elephants, tigers, gorillas, wolves, bears, dolphins, turtles and many more species in their natural habitat,

Find out more at *www.bornfree.org.uk*

Contents

Years 9–11

Foreword

When I was a little girl I had two dreams. The first was that one day I would walk into a book shop and see a book with my name in it; I'd be a published author. And the second was that wild animals would be left alone to live as they should be – free. I would often write stories about this, about what it felt like to be a wild animal and what it would feel like if my freedom was stolen.

My first dream did come true. But the second is still a work in progress. It is why the Born Free Foundation works tirelessly to protect the world's wildlife, trying to pass new laws and trying to rescue animals that need their help. They believe that wild animals have the right to be left alone; not captured for zoos or wildlife parks or made to perform in circuses or dolphinariums. They firmly believe animals should be what they are meant to be, and live as they are meant to live.

I share the same belief which is why I set up Paws n Claws Publishing; to show how the written word can both inform and change the way we see animals, but also through the sale of every book we publish, to make a donation to help Born Free continue their valuable work.

Writing stories is a great way to develop empathy, which is the ability to be in someone or something else's skin, to think what they think and feel what they feel. This is why I set up PAWS, the Publishing & Writing Animal Workshop Scheme and why I visit schools and encourage children to explore the emotional lives of animals by writing about them. I believe that what we learn as children stays with us as adults and that includes how we feel about animals.

I always remember how proud I felt when I won an animal writing competition, aged ten, and saw my story published in a magazine. I wanted to give young writers the opportunity to feel the same as I did, but I also wanted to publish these stories in a book, something very special that would last forever. The 2011 Paws Writing Competition was open to children from as young as nine years old through to sixteen because I knew there was immense talent out there. And I was right.

Myself, my lovely team of preliminary judges and of course our prestigious judges, actress and founder of the Born Free charity, Virginia McKenna OBE, children's authors Alan Gibbons and Lauren St. John, were quite literally bowled over by the standard of the stories. Even those stories that didn't make it into the book will be on our website later this year.

The twenty-eight stories you will read here are the judges' final shortlist including of course the winner and runner-up in each of the three age categories. Some of the other stories also get a special mention from the judges. We later asked all the children that entered the competition to send drawings to illustrate some of the stories and you'll see these too – again what talent! We have stories and drawings by children from England, Wales, Scotland, France and even South Africa.

What all the stories show is not only a talent for writing, and who knows this might be the start of a writing career for some, but also how much they all understood the message of the book. So this special collection is dedicated to the world's wildlife and to The Born Free Foundation. The message is the same as that dream I had when I was a little girl: that one day all wild animals will be born, will live and will stay free… *wild n free.*

Debz

Debz Hobbs-Wyatt is a full time fiction writer, editor and publisher working from her home in the mountains of Snowdonia in Wales. She lives with her cats Cagney and Lacey and her mad cocker spaniel, Rosie. She originally trained and worked as a scientist and has an MSc in Ecology, she has always been passionate about animals. She now has her MA in Creative Writing and works with a lot of developing writers including running PAWS workshops in schools.

Debz has had several short stories published and written four novels. She is also an Editor and Publicist for Bridge House Publishing, short story specialists, Editor for CaféLit an online short story community, and the founder of Paws n Claws Publishing. She writes a daily blog for developing writers.

Useful links

www.debzhobbs-wyatt.co.uk
Twitter: @PawsDebz
Writing Blog: *http://wordznerd.wordpress.com/*
www.pawsnclawspublishing.co.uk
www.thejet-set.com

Years 5 and 6

A note from our judge, Virginia McKenna OBE

Co-Founder and Trustee of international wildlife charity the Born Free Foundation, Virginia McKenna is a renowned actress best known with her husband Bill Travers for their roles in *Born Free*. The true story of Elsa the lioness sparked her lifelong commitment to wildlife. Virginia McKenna's long career as an actress includes *The Cruel Sea*, *Carve Her Name with Pride* and *A Town Like Alice*, and the stage musical *The King and I*.

Whilst Virginia still works occasionally as an actress, her priority is the plight of wild animals. Her memoirs *The Life in My Years* (2009) were published to great acclaim, and she was voted one of the most inspirational people of all time in a *Daily Telegraph* poll.

She was delighted to be asked to be one of the judges in the Paws Competition and made the final selection from the Years 5 and 6 stories.

"All the stories I was sent to read were fascinating, original, and evidence that the 'short story' can have as great an impact as a longer one. It was extremely difficult to select a 'winner' and a 'runner up'. I first isolated four stories, 'The Only True Enemy is Man'; 'How the Meerkat Got its Marks'; 'The Poacher that Called a Panther a Friend'; and 'Wolf Story'. I read each of these three times. In the end I selected two – 'The Poacher that Called a Panther a Friend' and 'The Only

True Enemy is Man'. But which was the 'winner'?

Both are exceptional and the latter has an unusual, extraordinary and quite profound ending. Both describe life and experiences from the animal's point of view. It was a dilemma!

Then I knew I was strongly drawn to 'The Poacher that Called a Panther a Friend'. It is quite sophisticated, very aware of the nature of both humans and animals. It is succinct, economical and completely original in concept. I have never read a story quite like it.

So – my congratulations to the authors of both stories and to the ten others who, I am delighted have also been published. All are worthy of this. So, in a way, everyone is a winner."

Winning Story Years 5 and 6

Miranda Lee

The Poacher that called a Panther a Friend

The panther picks out a strange smell and investigates. He's cautious at first as he knows poachers have been nearby and is scared of traps. He doesn't want to be injured. If he can't hunt, he can't feed. He finds a strange thing in the roots of an old tree. It's shiny, smooth, harder than rock and doesn't move.

It's not prey.

It's a jewel, but he doesn't have the human word for it yet. He bats it with a paw.

Suddenly he feels his body changing.

His face becomes flatter, his shoulders and spine pull upright, his back legs lengthen, his front paws develop opposable thumbs. He shakes and his fur slides off as if he's shaking off water. He doesn't feel pain, but feels different. He is muscular and graceful in movement. Two legs and only having faint hairs on his skin feels odd. So do the things he can feel against his skin, like skin but not part of his skin. Later he learns he is wearing a tee shirt and jeans, has coal-black hair and amber eyes. His skin is the colour of sun-bleached mud. He goes back to his cave for shelter. He'd eaten on the day he changed so doesn't feel hungry. Not yet.

Later he comes across the camp of humans. One takes

pity on him and offers food. Cooked meat still tastes like meat, but he avoids the green stuff the humans eat as well. The human talks to him but he doesn't really listen as he's distracted by the smell. This human smells like the poacher. He thinks this human is the poacher so asks about hunting. The poacher tells him they hunt to eat and kill other predators because they kill the animals they keep for food. He thinks about this. He only kills to eat. But the humans kill other hunters. Humans keep animals to eat and kill more than they need. This doesn't seem balanced. The poacher calls him friend. He doesn't know what a friend is but the poacher smiles. He finds being a human confusing as humans prefer to spend time in groups rather than alone. They cut the day up into twenty-four segments and do things in the right segment, not by the movement of the sun or by the weather.

He uses the jewel to turn back into a panther, so he can hunt again. But he's not the only one out hunting. Not quite used to his panther senses again, he doesn't realise how close the human is until he's shot. He feels pain burn through his outer ear. He stalks off to safety.

In his cave, he knows from smell that the shooter was the poacher who called him friend. The shot made a hole in his outer ear but didn't do any serious damage. The poacher didn't recognise him, didn't know he'd shot his friend. The panther decides to leave the jewel alone. The poacher doesn't deserve his friendship.

About the author

Miranda Lee started watching Big Cat Diary when she was nine months old because Mum was bored of looking at a cat picture book and started flicking through TV channels. Miranda has adopted big cats, including a lioness through Born Free. A daughter of two poets, she wants to be an inventor when she grows up, but might consider being a writer as well because writers invent stories. Miranda lives in Leicester with her mum and cat, Honey, and goes to Fernvale Primary School.

The Poacher that called a Panther a Friend is dedicated to Dad, who passed away last year.

Drawing: 'Panther' by the author, Miranda Lee

Runner-up

Charlotte Ash

The Only True Enemy is Man

I ran.

The trees blurred, the grass blurred, everything blurred. I ran. Fox was a streak of glistening red fur. I ran. He opened his gleaming white jaws, his eyes shone with malice and excitement. He knew that this was the end. He knew that he'd caught me this time. He knew that there was no escape. His teeth snapped together. I felt pain run through me, like liquid fire. But still, I ran. A black hole opened up in front of me. I loped towards it, relief flooding through me as I embraced death. I heard Fox's howl of rage. I felt myself falling, falling, falling…

But wait!

Was this death?

I slowly opened an eye, and saw a tiny face, staring at me anxiously.

"Daddy?" asked the little face, nervously.

I opened the other eye, and saw my wife, her eyes full of concern. I turned my head, and saw my three small daughters, scared and hungry. I felt tears run down my cheeks. They wanted food, they needed food, and I had failed them. I had nothing.

I felt a sharp pain in my left ear. My wife was binding the torn stub in oak leaves.

"Bed," I said weakly, to my son and daughters. I saw their fluffy tails bobbing as they scampered off. My wife helped me into a chair. I looked around my warren. I twitched my whiskers. Just minutes ago, I had thought that I would never see it again.

"Fox has never got this close to killing me before," I murmured. "And now he knows where the warren is. We need to move it, but we are too weak. We need food, but I am too weak to go and get some. If I try, this time Fox will kill me."

"There is nothing you can do, Dear. It is not your fault. Now, sleep. You will need it."

***

He carefully set out the trap.

"Are you sure about this, Dave?" asked his partner, in his whining, nasal voice.

"Yes," grated Dave, "shut up, Alan."

Alan looked sulky. Dave claimed to have seen a fox here, earlier. He said it had been chasing a rabbit, but Alan didn't trust him. Dave and Alan were poachers, so foxes and rabbits meant a good meal and fur to sell. Alan sighed, picked up his gun and climbed into a nearby bush.

***

The young rabbit listened to his parents talking.

When he heard them go to bed, he came to a decision. He crept out of his bedroom and up out of the warren. His family needed food; his family would get food. He crossed the barren field, and sneaked into Fox's territory. He nibbled the lush green grass and sighed with pleasure. Suddenly he heard a snap.

"And what," growled Fox, "do you think you're doing?"

All of a sudden, there was a deafening boom, and Fox

collapsed. The rabbit ran into a bush, terrified, as two humans rushed over to Fox with a cage. They whooped and cackled with glee, as they set the cage down and lit a fire. They ate some beans that they heated over the campfire, then fell asleep beside the slowly dying flames.

***

Fox's leg hurt. The humans had shot him. Fox had lost all hope when he saw the bars around him, and now he lay there, alone, dying...

"Psst!"

Fox turned his head, and saw the tiny rabbit.

"What?" muttered Fox.

"I'm going to try and rescue you. Be ready to run."

"But why? I'm the enemy!"

"No," said the young rabbit, "the only true enemy is Man."

The rabbit climbed onto the bigger man's shoulder and untied the key from round his neck.

He hopped over to Fox's cage, and unlocked it.

"Run!"

***

I woke up and immediately knew something was wrong. My son's bed was empty! I rushed outside and my fears were confirmed. He was nowhere in sight. He had gone to find food. I no longer cared about being spotted by Fox, I had to find my son before it was too late. I hopped up the rocky hill to look out over Fox's valley. But at the top, was Fox, and with him was my son.

***

The small rabbit followed Fox up a rocky hill.

"Thank you," said Fox, simply, "if you ever want food, just come and take it. I won't chase you, I owe you my life."

But then something terrible happened.

***

So this is my situation, and I can only think of one solution. A life for a life. My life for my son's. I take a deep breath, and throw myself at Fox, my lifelong nemesis. So this is the end.

For both of us.

***

Fox barely had time to register the fact that he was falling, before he hit the rocks below.

"Goodbye, old friend," he whispered, as darkness stole over him. As he watched the light go out in the old rabbit's eyes, Fox sighed softly, and died.

About the author

Charlotte Ash comes from Leamington Spa, but is currently going to school in France. She loves animals and has an

'The Fox and The Rabbit' by the author, Charlotte Ash

unnaturally clever hamster called Livvi, who has already discovered that she can open her cage from the *inside*.

Charlotte believes that animals and humans should live alongside one another with mutual respect... but she does like chicken curry.

This story is dedicated to Burnard, a beautiful but very grumpy black and white rabbit who breathed his last in September 2010, bravely battling a savage dog to the bitter end, therefore providing the inspiration for *The Only True Enemy is Man*.

Look out for a few of Charlotte's drawings throughout the book as well!

Highly Commended

Thomas Sherlock

How the Meerkat Got its Marks

Long ago, before any man had crossed the scorching sands of the Kalahari, the Sun God was soaring above the desert in his winged chariot. He was hunting for a magical pearl to drop on the desert drought and to form a fresh, new oasis. The land had been parched for months and all creation had been aching for a deluge. The Sun God wanted to make sure that a good mix of creatures could survive in the lands that he watched over.

However, one of the desert-dwellers was much more selfish and vain than all the rest. A white-feathered, long necked bird, which we now call "the flamingo" was out to steal the magic pearl for herself. She wanted to use it to make a small private pool so she could gaze at her reflection forever.

Just as the God had caught a glimpse of the pearl glinting in the desert, he saw Flamingo swoop down, pick it up in her strong, hooked bill and start to fly away. The Sun God was boiling with rage and sped after her. As his anger increased, so did the speed of his chariot. If anyone had been watching, all that they would have seen was a blur of burnished gold, a second sun in the sky.

He let loose a great ball of bright flame, which missed Flamingo and hit a nearby meerkat burrow. It was as dry as kindling and quickly caught fire. As the flames took hold, the terrified meerkats squealed and tried to scramble out. Panicking, they toppled over one another like blocks in a game of Jenga. Only one of the mob managed to get to the surface; all the rest were beaten back by the flames, choked on the smoke and slid desperately back down again.

The one brave escapee was determined to save his family and friends. He sniffed the cinders and soil to get their scent. He cupped his ear to the burrow's mouth to listen for their calling and crying. Then he slid his tail down the hole and screamed to his relations to "Bite on to it! Bite onto it!"

One by one, he pulled them all to safety.

When he had finished the rescue, the end of his poor tail was blackened with bruises. His ears and snout were stained by the ash. He rubbed his two tired eyes with his paws. He didn't notice how sooty they had become and that he had made big black smudges round his eyes.

Meanwhile, the Sun God had hit Flamingo with a volley of flames, turning her eyes a startling orange and her feathers a ferocious pink. The God decreed that, as a punishment for her selfishness and vanity, all flamingos would from thereon after have that colouring.

He also proclaimed that, in recognition of one meerkat's bravery and selflessness, all creatures of that kind would have black tail-tips, eye-patches, noses and inner ears. They would be marked in that way from that day to the end of eternity.

About the author

Thomas Sherlock is 11 and lives with his parents, his twin sisters, his guinea pig Scruffy and more than twenty toy meerkats in Hertfordshire. He currently attends Beechwood Park School but will be moving to Haberdashers' Aske's School for Boys in September. He has loved books and reading for as long as he can remember and more recently has enjoyed writing stories, articles and poems. He loves classic cars, football and meerkats!

Paws for Thought Discussion Point

We did not receive any drawings of meerkats, but might we suggest you have a look at some photographs, in books and websites and look for the markings Thomas has told us about. Do you see them? Why might they be that colour do you think? Does an animal's colour help it survive? How?

Highly Commended

Morgan Joy Ashby
Wolf Story

The pack tear the meat off the small, scrawny deer, tossing chunks into the air and catching them in their strong ravenous jaws.

All the trees are bare, it was a harsh winter and the two-legs were taking their food. They live in a pine forest at the foot of the mountains, with the wide, shallow river flowing through the heart of it.

This is their last meal. There are no deer left and the wolves will starve.

The alpha-male's instincts tell him they must go up to find new territory in the high snowy mountains but he has never been there.

He must put away his pride and ask the old wise wolf, who had lived there as a cub. The old wolf is pure white like a glacier and once held his tail and ears higher than them all. Alpha hasn't spoken to him since the fight.

Alpha goes to the old wolf and rolls on his back exposing his belly. Glacier howls: "Follow the river upstream."

But they can't go yet because Silvina's body is large and full of squirming cubs, ready to scrabble out.

They need a den quickly because the two-legs are coming with the sun.

***

In an underground den, under the roots of a twisted old yew, six strong healthy cubs are born, they are blind and helpless. As Silvina licks warmth into them, a tiny seventh cub appears.

Will she have enough milk without food? Twelve searches now and no more deer.

The snow is quickly melting and flooding the river. On the thirteenth hunt, the pack is famished and feeling it's the end of the world. Weaklings are in great danger of getting swept away. Swept down by the strong current, they manage to scrabble up onto a wrecked beaver's dam and find a family of beavers to eat.

Surviving on frequent snacks of small mammals, such as drowned hares and squirrels, the pack care for the cubs. Silvina gives them milk and then after six weeks her sisters help sick up chewed meat for them too.

***

A terrible great noise vibrates the whole forest. Chainsaws are cutting down trees. Even though the cubs are too small they must set off now or the two-legs will destroy everything.

Glacier howls: "I will hold back the two-legs. It is time for you to go. May the spirit of the Black Wolf be in you, guard you, and give you strength. Remember the important thing is teamwork."

***

They set off running through the tree stumps, jumping over fallen branches and dodging falling trees.

Running from the falling trees.

Running in fear.

Glacier growls, snarls and reveals his sharp crystal white canine fangs.

The pack gets away.

***

The cubs struggle to keep up. The runt is badly lagging behind. She can smell the two-legs behind her but suddenly Silvina grabs her by the scruff of her neck and carries her off in her jaws.

Drawing by Neelai Patel

They follow the river upstream. The new lush spring grass feels soft under their sore paws. They keep going, only stopping for a drink when they are far from the forest, high in the steep rocks.

A cougar leaps down from a rock to attack, aiming to pick off the runt, but the rest of the pack snarl and snap, defending her.

But then an eagle swoops down. They leave the path of

the stream taking a detour into the bushes for cover.

They are feeling relieved that they are far from the two-legs and that the whole pack has escaped the cougar and the eagle, without a scratch. They must be near the top of the snowy mountain.

They can feel the chill in the air. They can smell deer.

In the dense bushes they get stuck in deep thorns and can't find a way out. They can smell the stream. Downhearted after all their efforts to find new territory, they cannot believe it will end like this. Alpha holds his ears and tail low. He has failed as a leader. Silvina licks and nuzzles her cubs.

Hearing the last long howl of Glacier, the little runt gets a sudden burst of energy and breaks through a minute chink in the tangled dense thorns with the strength of the Black Wolf.

Herds of deer at the mountain spring in the shining sun at the top of the mountain. The wolves claim their new paradise territory, howling with joy.

About the author

Morgan Joy Ashby loves nature, especially beaches, woods, mud and horses! She reads everything from Ancient History and Cosmology to the Beano! She is the Ted Hughes Poet of the Year (youngest section) and her poems and illustrations have been published. Her art has also been exhibited and she likes optical illusions and 3D art best.

About the artist

Neelai is a 12-year-old boy who lives in London. He has spent his whole life with his parents, brother and grandparents. Neelai collects many things such as key rings, rocks and something very unusual, sand! He likes drawing and colouring because he can let his imagination run wild and be experimental with his work. Neelai also loves to see his finished piece, good or bad! He loves to play the guitar and the drums and his favourite sports are tennis, football, hockey and table tennis. He is thrilled for his drawing to be published in this book as it is a great achievement.

Luke Julier

The Clever Chameleon

Long, long ago in an African reserve, deep in the heart of Africa, there lived a chameleon that didn't fit in. He was always left out and he thought he was useless. He was actually very clever as he could change to any colour whenever he wished. If he sat on a tree, he was brown. If he sat on a leaf, he turned green, but he was lonely and sad as no one knew he was there. He had no friends or anyone to play with.

He decided to go and see the king of the reserve. The king was the fiercest lion in all of Africa. "Oh Mr Lion," he said in a nervous voice, "I wish I had a loud roar like you, I can only change colour."

"Oh you will never have the loudest roar," laughed the lion. "You're just a silly little chameleon. You're useless."

The chameleon walked away sadly.

***

The next morning he went looking for the elephant. He was taking a bath in the warm clear river. "Mr Elephant, I wish I had ears like you," cried the chameleon, "all I can do is change colour and no one ever notices me."

"Oh you will never have ears like me," laughed the elephant. "I can hear for miles, you're just a silly chameleon."

17

The elephant went off laughing and left the sad little chameleon sitting by the riverside all alone.

At sunset the chameleon was sitting on a tree when a whoosh of yellow and black zoomed past him, it was leopard. The leopard had a long tail and dotted skin.

"Oh Mr Leopard I wish I could run as fast as you," said the chameleon sadly. The leopard could go 70 mph but the chameleon could only creep along slowly.

"Oh you will never be able to be as fast as me," laughed the leopard. He zoomed off into the sunset and left chameleon all by himself again.

***

The next morning the chameleon went looking for a strange animal called Mr Anteater, he had a long nose so he had a great sense of smell. He found Mr Anteater eating ants at a cliff side.

"Mr Anteater," said the Chameleon. "I wish I had a sense of smell like you."

Mr Anteater looked at him and said, "You will never be like me with that tiny little nose. Go away before I trample over you."

The chameleon set off rather quickly on his way home. He was still sad, very lonely and now a little bit scared.

As he wandered through the deserts, alone and sad, he heard a strange sound. It was a loud, banging, and exploding sound. Something he had never heard before. Suddenly the lion, anteater, leopard and elephant came running past. They didn't even see the chameleon, camouflaged in the sand.

The sounds were guns and they were fired by poachers. The animals were all running away.

What could Chameleon do? He was so small and

helpless. He then had an idea. Chameleon shouted as they ran by "Lion hide in the tallest rocks, Leopard hide in the tallest grass, Elephant hide in the warm river, Anteater hide in the deepest holes."

They were all so scared that they listened to the little chameleon and all ran to where he had told them to go.

The Poachers couldn't find them.

They gave up and went home.

After a while the animals crept out of their hiding places; all safe, but scared. They all thanked Chameleon for being so clever and saving them. They were sorry for being so mean to him and for making him feel so small and useless when really he was the most cleverest animal in Africa.

From that day on everyone respected the chameleon and remembered he was there even when they couldn't see him.

About the author

Luke Julier is a student at East Farleigh Primary School in Maidstone, Kent and lives with his mum, dad, brother and cocker spaniel Jasper. He really enjoys writing and art because both topics fill his head with amazing ideas and wonderful images. Luke is overwhelmed to have his story published. Luke finds animals beautiful and fascinating and enjoys writing about them. Luke's hobby is playing football at the weekend for West Farleigh FC.

Luke dedicates his story to his younger brother Harry, his cocker spaniel Jasper, and to all at East Farleigh Primary School.

Paws for Thought Discussion Point

Here is a drawing of a chameleon...

What, you don't see it? Maybe it's so well camouflaged it's turned white and invisible! These are very clever animals, so do see if you can look them up and find out more about them. Perhaps you might explore the role of camouflage as an aid to survival and look at how the chameleon has taken this a step further by being able to change its colour to match its surroundings. How does the chameleon change colour?

Sachin Tankaria

The Humble Fox

Deep in the Savannah Grasslands of the Sub Saharan region of Africa, there was a lioness. Her Toblerone nose stood proudly out towards her cubs. Her jade eyes shimmered reflecting the twilight sunset. Her whiskers were as white as snow and as soft as silk. She stood taking in the warmth of the day, with her cubs close by shadowing her graceful movements. They peered at her with excitement of what she had brought back from the hunt with her today.

They had been lucky lately of being fed a great feast of hearty succulent juicy red meat. Some days there would be very little to go around.

***

This evening, like every evening, the lioness would leave her cubs with the meat from her hunt. The feverishly hungry cubs bit and tore the meat like savages, unaware of their surroundings; their feast was interrupted by unfamiliar footsteps.

They froze in unison while a richly golden fox stealthily crept up to the cubs and admired them. The fox's mouth watered at the sight and smell of the last piece of shredded meat displayed within his grasp. Like a flash of light, he snapped his mouth and grabbed it. The cubs huddled

21

together motionless awaiting the fox's next move. The fox proudly just walked away with his findings tightly grasped between his jaws.

The lioness tiresomely hunted for the cub's food night after night, each day leaving her cubs with her hunted meat, and each night the fox returning for his share. The lioness struggled to feed what she thought was her growing army of hungry cubs, unknowing that she was also providing for a lazy devious fox.

***

One hot evening after the lioness presented her cubs with her hunted meat, she left them as she always did except this time she hadn't gone too far before feeling exhausted. She stopped for a well-earned rest. She fought her tired eyes but eventually gave in to sleep.

Meanwhile, like clockwork, the fox came along so confident now of his routine; he was unaware of the noise his footsteps were making. The cubs too were used to his visit by now and weren't so shocked by him. The lioness however was not used to visitors and was woken with the first sound of scrunching footsteps on the leaves. She instantly rushed to her den to find the fox with a great piece of succulent meat held in between his teeth.

She pounced on him while her claw caught his flesh but he managed to slide under her and run away with all his might. The lioness chased him but her tired body caught up with her, she eventually lost trail and returned to the den.

The lioness watched her cubs and took a moment to understand the situation. From then on she changed her routine, always aware of the fox but he did not return. The cubs and lioness had almost forgotten about him and went about their lives undisturbed for many weeks.

***

Drawing by Charlotte Ash

One late morning the lioness strolled off leaving the cubs playing in their den, it wasn't long after that the den was discovered by another unexpected creature, this time, though, the cubs were being attacked by a raging striped hyena.

The cubs were running around frantically not knowing which direction was safe. Before they knew it the fox appeared, he crept up to the hyena silently and stabbed his dagger-like claws into her. The hyena screeched and screamed. The fox then bit the hyena ravenously. The noise of the hyena sent the lioness galloping to her cubs, where she witnessed the fox fighting for her young. The hyena realised the presence of the lioness and retreated wounded into the woods.

The fox and lioness stood facing one another about a hundred feet away staring at each other cautiously. The fox stood as still as he could even though his hind leg was covered in blood from his recent struggle. The fox was no match for the lioness, she could finish him off with one blow. And he knew it. But he waited patiently for a reaction from her. The lioness eventually turned away and strolled to her cubs while the fox slowly crept away towards the woods.

***

Thereafter, the lioness carried on her duties to feed her young. She went on hunting, sometimes for enough food for her cubs and other times for a little bit more. She never saw the fox again but she knew that she wasn't always just feeding her cubs; she knew that her cubs had a visitor now and again but she pretended to be unaware. Every now and again she looked into the woods thankfully; she knew that her young ones would always be safe.

About the author

Sachin Tankaria lives in North-West London. He lives with his mum, dad, brother and sister. He wrote this story when he was in St. Martins, Northwood but now he is at a high school called Haberdashers' Aske's Boys' School. Sachin likes animals because he likes the fact that he lives with loads of other creatures, some not yet discovered, and that they all live in one small place, the Earth. It means quite a lot to him to be published in this book as it is a fundraiser to help all needy animals.

Sachin likes to collect Glass ornaments of landmarks of all the countries he has been to. He likes to visit lots of different countries.

Sachin dedicates this story to Mango, his very loved pet rabbit who was eaten by a fox, and to James, his other much loved pet rabbit who escaped from the rabbit hutch and ran away.

Thomas Bailey

Life in the Bamboo Forests of China

Tramp, tramp, tramp, came the footsteps of the beast. Its innocent eyes peered out from the dense, lime-green ferns. The craving for bamboo surged through his mind once more. His soft and sooty fur was visible in the bright sunlight. His silky, furry paws touched the muddy ground, leaving wet footprints on the surface. The Giant Panda scooped up all the delicious bamboo he could find.

As he sat down on his hind legs, he felt a raindrop trickling down his triangular jet-black nose. He watched in awe at the drop of water on his fur, and then looked up.

The sunlight was fading, and slate-grey clouds were beginning to form. Rumble! came the thunder. Crackle! came the lightning. The rain was now pelting down through the thick undergrowth, sliding down and dripping off the large leaves of the forest. The elegant raindrops sparkled as they burst.

***

The Giant Panda hid behind the lime-green ferns, protecting itself from the harsh rain. Subtle flashes of jagged lightning reached out like claws from the steel sky. He watched the endless monsoon through the night, dozing off peacefully.

***

As he woke, he heard the screeching calls of the rare Crested Ibis. The group of birds scattered as a sound approached. He recognised it immediately – the frightening sound of a poacher's gunshot.

The Giant Panda had heard this terrifying sound when he was a cub – the time when he had found a group of lifeless deer in a boggy marsh. He certainly did not want to be like those deer.

He tried to camouflage himself from the menacing sound, hiding behind the luxuriant ferns and tall, large bamboo stalks in the impenetrable undergrowth of nettles and brambles.

The shouting voices and loud gunshots came to a climax when the poachers had reached the very spot where he was hiding. He kept as still as a statue in the heavy undergrowth.

The two men both had straight, dark hair, each wearing a tattered hat, a khaki jacket, with a sweaty, blood-red scarf tied around their necks. One carried a 22-caliber Rimfire Rifle, while the other muscular one slung the dead animals over his left shoulder.

The poachers had stopped right outside his den. They must have realised something. Then he heard one of the men loading the rifle. He cowered in his hiding place, holding his breath.

Time passed as slowly as the grass growing in the forest clearings, seeming like hours. He kept his place in the tightly packed undergrowth, watching the raven-black shadows shift.

***

Bang!

The first man must have shot an innocent deer in the

gut which was just passing by, because the animal jumped up and reared with an arched body. The poachers moved on, unaware of his presence.

The Panda was safe, but for how long?

***

It was now late April, and the Giant Panda had another problem on his paws – finding a mate. He had been unsuccessful last year, but would he be able to find one this year?

He stalked the never-ending bamboo forest, looking for a female. He needed to find one, and fast, because the end of the breeding season was mid-May. This was in exactly a fortnight.

In the last week of the mating season, he spotted an unusual shape on the horizon, slowly lumbering towards his territory. He noticed the recognisable silk and velvet markings with the same triangular nose and ebony pointed ears. He had finally found a female panda!

But this was not over – he had spotted more shapes of pandas in the distance. Unfortunately, these were males. If he wanted to help her conceive, he had to battle it out with the other strong males.

He took his place as the battle began. He knew he had to win this to help the female give birth. The panda he would be brawling with was a large one. He wondered if he would even get a chance to attack.

***

The battle began as the opposing panda reared and tore at his fur. Pain surged through his body, triggering thoughts of sweet revenge in his brain. He lunged and scraped at the other panda's fur, while biting both hind legs. The other panda reared in complete agony and fell onto the ground with a huge thud. The huge panda signalled that he had given up as he was now unable to get up.

He had won!

He had now got his first mate. Wondering what a joy fathering a cub would be like, he lay down on all four paws. He would just have to wait and see!

About the author

Thomas Bailey is a LEGO enthusiast from the suburbs of London, where he lives with his mum and dad. He wrote this story because his mum's family is originally from China and loves pandas. He likes LEGO because one can build virtually anything one wants.

Thomas believes animals should have rights and should be able to roam about in the wild safely. He wants to be a writer or a scientist when he grows up.

He dedicates this story to all pandas (in captivity and in the wild) and hopes they will all someday be free.

Paws for Thought Discussion Point

Sadly we don't have a picture of a panda for you but I'm sure you'll all be familiar with what these lovely animals look like. They're relatives of the bear and they live almost exclusively on bamboo shoots and leaves. There are considered to be less than a thousand left in the wild. Why are there so few?

Alex Cumming

Surprising Survival

The young animal, with its head down, staggered through the thick, sparkly snow, dragging its freezing feet along. Its raven black tail was drooping down sadly and the creature's body, which was covered in frosty fur, shivered in the bitter arctic wind. The wolf desperately needed to find its pack or it would starve to death.

The poor creature could remember two days ago when it was playing happily with its friends, running around in circles with clouds of powdery snow filling the air. A sudden deafening silence followed and made the wolf realise that its pack was gone.

Ever since then, the weary looking animal had been frantically looking for its lost family and some food.

Suddenly the wolf froze.

Its pointed ears pricked up. It could just hear crunching noises in the icy snow and smell a moose. The ravenous mammal instantly knew that this was its only chance. The wolf silently crept with its cotton wool paws deeper into dense forest following the sound until it could see a chestnut brown figure through the branches of a spruce tree, covered in heavy layers of white snow. The pain in the wolf's stomach had become unbearable as thick saliva poured down the sides of its mouth. All the wolf could think about was a chunk of warm and juicy moose's meat.

The inexperienced creature could not stop itself from charging on its own at a moose calf, unaware of the looming danger. The wolf stretched its thin body like a strong spring and pounced with all its might at the young moose. Just as it was about to sink its teeth in the calf's neck it felt a sudden and excruciating pain at the side of its ribs. The piercing, spine-tingling, howling noise of the wounded animal filled the air as the wolf's body hit hard on the icy ground. The tops of tall trees were spinning like a merry-go-round in front of the half closed eyes of the confused creature. The wolf could just make out the furious face of mother moose glaring at him. It closed its eyes in terror and prepared itself for certain death.

As the weak animal lay powerlessly it could hear the quick clattering of hooves and the sound of rustling bushes disappearing in the distance. The wolf opened its eyes only to see a dark figure walk towards it. The hunter quickly pointed a silver gun at the creature's chest. The poor animal's heart started pounding like a hammer as it

'Wolf' by the author Alex Cumming

tried to pull itself up to run away. The wolf's shaky legs gave way and as it turned its head towards the human the creature's blazing, hopeless red eyes interlocked with the hunter's.

The wolf could just pick out a hint of pity in the hunter's cold stare.

The native Alaskan lowered his gun, turned round and shuffled away through the shiny thick snow leaving deep footprints.

Suddenly a familiar howling sound spread through the wintry forest.

About the author

Alex Cumming is an 11-year-old boy who lives with his mum, dad and a younger brother in Rickmansworth, Hertfordshire. He is a pupil of St Martin's School in Northwood where he was able to develop creative writing skills under a watchful eye of his English teacher, Ms Flynn. He loves art, reading, sleepovers, playing on his X-Box and sharing good jokes with his school friends.

Although currently he does not have a pet, Alex has promised to help look after a tortoise his brother is planning to buy.

Alex likes to read fantasy, adventure books such as Harry Potter and Percy Jackson.

Eleanor Thornton

The Great Squirrel Rescue

Hi, I'm Sammy Squirrel and I am going to tell you about an out-of-the ordinary experience with my brother Stanley, my two sisters Sally and Samantha and a horrible boy! Ha, we sure showed him!

***

It was the first day of spring when I love going out of the hollow in our Elm tree and watching all the insects. Benny Bee and I are very good friends.

This morning I watched the rabbit family, who had been hibernating over the winter, come out. After that my brother, my two sisters and I were feeling rather peckish so Mum took us to get breakfast.

The ideal place for a snack is below the green bird feeder that hangs on the wall. It is too small for us to actually collect seeds from the feeder, so we busied ourselves picking up what the birds had dropped.

Whilst we had breakfast we talked about the old cottage across the road. A few months ago the old couple who'd lived there moved out and ever since then there had been a *For Sale* sign up. We didn't give it much thought until the sign was removed and a *Sold* sign stood in its place.

Anyway, after breakfast the four of us went and collected some moss and feathers to line the floor. Whilst

Stanley and I wove carpets and blankets out of grass, our sisters got creative with some flowers. Soon the hollow was filled with lovely smells. The walls were covered in daisy chains and snowdrops and daffodils covered the floor. Any boys out there who think that's bad, should see what it's like when bluebells come out...

It was almost lunchtime and as we went to go and collect some lunch, a big lorry pulled up and some strange men started moving furniture into the old house. For two days the unloading carried on and then a family finally arrived.

There was a man who was tall with dark brown hair and a hat. His skin was pale and he wore a white T-shirt with blue trousers. Beside him trotted a woman who wore a short pink dress and pink high-heels. She had blonde hair swept into a bun and she carried a little white shoulder bag. Sagging on behind them was the most peculiar boy you could ever meet. He had scruffy brown hair and a scowl that could turn the milk sour. He had a red T-shirt saying *Killer* on it and saggy black trousers. His trainers were brown and scuffed. Overall he was not the type of boy you would wish to be around.

***

Over time we learned that the boy's name was Billy and that he was as scruffy inside as he was out. Most of the time he hung around near our Elm tree tearing down branches and throwing stones at birds. Once we even saw him setting a trap for rabbits. Luckily it was hopelessly built. We would drop nuts on his head to distract him but one time I suppose we got a bit careless and he spotted us. Samantha ran back into our hollow in a panic which showed him where we lived. We stood very still and heard him swear and curse plotting his revenge.

We hoped he would forget it but we were VERY wrong!

***

The next day he climbed up to the point of our hollow and stuck his hand in it! When his finger brushed over Stanley, Stanley twisted to bite him. Billy screamed and started blubbering like a baby. We rolled on the floor laughing at him squealing and crying! When he got to the floor he (again) swore revenge and ran off.

After we had stopped laughing we realised that this was serious and we really had to do something about it. The best place to work that out was Billy's room. It might be dangerous but we could find clues about his plans.

So, later on that day, we climbed up the drainpipe until we reached his window which was luckily open. It was easy to tell which bedroom was his because, as you can imagine, his bedroom was exactly like him. You couldn't see the floor; it was cluttered up with posters, sweet wrappers and other items of unnecessary junk. The bed was a blood-red colour with KILLER streaked across it. The desk was littered with scrunched up pieces of paper, pens and pins.

On top of a messy pile of comics I spotted an open notebook. On one page there was a drawing of what I think was supposed to be a squirrel only it was a stick man with pointy ears and a bushy tail and there was a big red cross on it. On the other page was written… *Trap a squirrel and put it in a cage.*

We looked at each other in horror.

We were just about to start shimmying down the drainpipe when Sally pricked up her ears and whispered in a panicked tone, "He's coming, let's get out of here quick!"

In our rush, Stanley, who was last out, slipped over a pen and fell down into an empty shoebox. I urged him to hurry up but he must have been in quite a daze because before we knew it, Billy had slammed the lid down over him and smiled an evil grin! And before we could get to the box Billy shut the window!

The rascal! The traitor! The, the… never mind.

We HAD to save Stanley.

***

We figured out that the best time to carry out any plan was when Billy was asleep. Well, the plan was basic. Get in, release Stanley and get the heck out of there!

We first had to tell Mum. She said that I could go but the two girls had to stay. I'm surprised that she let any of us go! Then again I'm going to be a spy squirrel when I grow up, like Dad. I've already started training and Mum says it will be good practice. The secret government order of the squirrels often does a lot of saving.

So, that evening about an hour after I saw Billy's light go out in the window, I snuck up the drainpipe to find a closed window. Typical!

I then scampered over to Billy's parents' room and luckily their window and door were open. I climbed through the window and round to Billy's closed door. Slipping under the door was no problem.

I looked around for the shoebox and saw one enclosed by a large metal colander and weighted down by a dirty pair of boots. So even if Stanley managed to chew through the shoebox, he still couldn't get free!

***

I ran over and pushed off the boots as quietly as possible. Then I managed to lift the colander and opened the lid of the box to see Stanley looking very miserable with life.

"Come on let's get out of here!" I whispered. We ran over to the door and were just about to slip under the gap when a large foot blocked our way. Billy!

Before I could move Billy grabbed me and said, "What you gonna do now?"

I didn't know until I saw the open notebook again. Had Billy ever heard us talk?

So, I opened my mouth and said, "Did you know the word squirrel has two Rs?"

He looked at me and stuttered, "The squirrel talked… why did the squirrel talk?"

And with that he dropped me and ran out of the room!

We opened the window and climbed to our hollow. It was a tearful reunion and apparently Sally and Samantha had had a bet. Sally thought we were gonners, and Samantha thought we would make it.

***

In the morning when Billy realised that he had been outwitted by a bunch of squirrels, he charged like a bull to our hollow and practically tore the place down. He only realised we weren't there when he saw a tiny *For Sale* sign. He was mad!

***

Stanley, Sally, Samantha and I watched him, laughing so hard our sides hurt, from our new home in a nearby Oak!

About the author

Eleanor Thornton lives in Wiltshire near Stonehenge. She lives with her mum, dad, her little brother Jack and her bonkers collie, Max. She goes to Farleigh School and absolutely loves writing. She is always having ideas but never has a chance to write them all down. She is thrilled that one of her stories will be published.

She loves collecting things such as bookmarks and funny shaped stones with her grandpa when they visit Westonbirt Arboretum.

She dedicates this story to a grey squirrel she always sees in her garden trying to get seeds from the bird feeder.

Paws for Thought Discussion Point

The grey squirrel gets a lot of bad press, but is it really the squirrel's fault? The grey squirrel was originally introduced to Britain from the United States over one hundred years ago. Any species not originally from a place is called an 'alien' species, as opposed to one that has always been there, called a 'native' species. The reason for the grey squirrel's bad press is that it is able to out-compete the native red squirrel for food. And this caused a massive drop in the number of red squirrels. The grey ones also carry a virus that killed a lot of red squirrels. There are projects now to try and save populations of red squirrels. But whatever you might think, all the grey squirrel is doing is what any wild animal is trying to do – survive. So if anyone is to blame for the depletion in the number of red squirrels, maybe it's us humans for introducing it to Britain in the first place. This is something you might like to think about and find out more about. What are your views?

Molli Tyldesley

Wolf Rescue

Foggy clouds scurried across the sky, the occasional fork of lightning lighting up the sheet of darkness spread across the world. Wispy fingers coiled themselves around me as I crept out into the forest.

My feet crunched on the cracked, dead leaves. Heart pounding in my chest, sweat trickling down my back, I ventured further into the towering trees. The remaining leaves whispered all around me, hissing secrets through the branches. Moonless nights like this were amazing. A mysteriously familiar feeling hung in the air, a sense of unknown happenings.

Somewhere in the distance there was a loud howl. Through the snow came footsteps, silently making their way towards me. Shaggy and wet, a tangled coat brushed against my legs, hurling a shiver down my spine. A sniffling nose like leather rubbed against my knee. I tore my eyes away from the ground and looked up at the wolf; its gleaming, bared teeth, its menacing though content eyes. Its powerful paws knocked me back and pinned me to the floor, digging in fiercely.

"Please don't hurt me," I whispered.

There was a low growling from the bushes – the wolf's ears pricked up like a dog's. Slowly, it scampered off into the forest, leaving me shocked and amazed. Dragging myself back to bed, I clambered in without changing, snow dripping down my back.

***

Sunlight streamed in through the window. It took a couple of minutes for my eyes to get used to the light and for my mind to remember the happenings of the night before. Had it really happened? I wasn't so sure. Never before had I sighted wolves in this forest – I never even dreamed of getting so close to one! Or maybe I had…

Maybe it snowed overnight, but when I got back down I searched high and low for the footprints made by the wolf. The curious thing was there was no trace of his, but a perfect line of mine, speeding down the path and into the thicker snow by the edge of the forest.

***

Three weeks later I had almost forgotten about the magnificent ordeal with the wolf, until of course, that angry pounding on the door – not a nice, polite knock, but a brutal slap on the hard oak. My grandfather frowned. Usually he spent the winter warming his toes by the fire, smoking his pipe whilst flicking through old newspapers.

"Now who could that be?" he grumbled. Sprawled across the floor surrounded by pencil crayons, I was drawing a picture of the wolf which I had not quite forgotten. By then I'd drawn exactly fifty-four pictures of him, each more faded and distant than the next.

When the door was swung open I knew it was not going to be good. Three sturdy men stood there, with bulging muscles and strained faces. Nervously their eyes darted about, as if spies were watching them from the old cabinets and rickety staircase.

"Mr Donavan?" asked the first. He was Canadian, so he must have lived nearby. I recognised him from the village.

Grandfather narrowed his eyes. "Whatever you want is no business of mine!" he snapped.

The second man coughed awkwardly. He stepped forward. "Are you sure about that, Sir?" he enquired, giving me a quizzical look. He leaned down and grasped my sketchbook, his eyes going wider, and his smile broader. "Little girl, have you seen any wolves around here?"

Glancing at my grandfather, I shook my head. "No, they've not been sighted for over thirty years."

Sighing, the men left. The man who'd found my sketchbook tossed it at my feet. At the last second he poked his head around the door. "If you know anything about that wolf, little girl, you better tell us. It is the most valuable animal in the world!"

They planned to hunt it, track it down and hunt it.

Disgusted, I picked up my sketchbook, smoothed down the pages and carried on drawing. Grandfather, who'd never been interested in my sketchbook or anything I ever did, looked at me carefully. "You do know something, don't you?"

I just smiled.

***

That night, when the moon hung in the sky like a searchlight scanning the world, I dressed quickly and slipped downstairs.

BANG!

Something crashed under my foot – I'd knocked over

the pile of art equipment. Grandfather continued snoring loudly, sniffling and talking in his sleep every now and then.

Once outside, breathing the smell of freedom, I tip-toed into the forest. Just as I was thinking how I was going to find the wolf and protect it from the hunters, there was a howl. Usually, I'd have been scared, but then I was relieved. An elated tingle flew through my body, like a mild electric shock, waking me up.

Racing towards the wolf, I saw it was not one, but three wolves! The enormous, muscular one I'd met some weeks ago, a delicate, graceful female wolf and a playful cub. Eyeing me carefully, they circled me like buzzards circling a zebra carcass, sniffing around.

If you've ever experienced the feel of liberty, like you are free, flying and swooping as you please, you'll understand how I felt. If you haven't, you've never lived. Suddenly a torch beam swept over us, blinding me. Shrieking and growling, the wolf family padded off, leaving me stranded. Closer now, I could make out the figure of four or so men, two of whom had visited our doorstep.

"Well, well, well! We meet again, I see – so you do know something about those wolves!" exploded one of them, looking displeased. "I think we've scared them off – but your little friends won't be alive for long. We've already caught one of the cubs!"

In the back of a battered old wagon, partially hidden in the bushes, a weak wolf cub was howling mournfully.

One of the evil men knocked on the cage. "SHUT UP!" he yelled.

The wolf cub fell silent, her eyes dull and empty.

Now I still don't know what made me do it. It was

one of the bravest, craziest things I've ever done. My hand shot out and next thing I know it made a quick but strong connection with somebody's nose. Blood covered, my fist pounded two more people, who fell stunned to the ground. Some of the others slunk back, but two of them came, rifles in hands. How I ever faced up to those burly men with eager-to-kill guns I'll never know.

With courage and determination flowing through my brain from my heart, I bashed them aside and fiddled with the rusty lock on the cage. Though it was old and the paint was flaking off, it was good at its job. Eventually I tugged it off and the timid, rigid wolf cub hobbled out,

'Wolf in the Forest' by Charlotte Ash

her bones stiff and feeble.

The rest of the men backed away, trundled off down the dusty road in the van. Hopefully they felt slightly scared. I turned to the baby wolf; she grinned up at me admiringly.

Unusually serene, her family emerged from the gloomy forest, looking sharp and not at all affected. Her mother licked her happily and they all ran off together. For a moment, the majestic father looked back, his eyes bright. Though I know it's impossible, probably a trick of the mind, I'm sure his eyes sparkled and then he winked a single, meaningful wink.

About the author

Molli Tyldesley lives in Manchester with her parents and younger brother. She goes to Light Oaks Junior School and wants to be a vet when she is older – though she also enjoys writing fiction. Molli wrote about a wolf because they are mysterious, powerful creatures, and myths are often told about them. Her other hobbies, besides writing and helping animals, are tae kwon do and netball.

She would like to dedicate her story to Fluffy, her rabbit, who recently died and was her first pet.

Daniel Maltz

The Emperor Penguin

The sleek Emperor Penguin stood, ready to dive. His soft black and white feathers ruffled in the breeze. With his pitch black eyes he could see the movement of fish swimming gracefully in the crystal clear water.

Deftly he dived, making hardly a splash. Swiftly he swam towards the fish, like a missile shooting through the water. He had already caught six fish by the time he caught sight of a massive, glistening fish. He caught another smaller one in his beak, hardly noticing it as it slipped down his throat. He was going for the big one. The fish was about thrice the size of the penguin's usual meal. It had bright yellow scales, which caught the light when it moved, tempting the hungry penguin.

But just as the Emperor penguin was about to catch

Drawing by the author, Daniel Maltz

it, the fish skilfully darted out of the way. Just as he spun around to try to give chase, he saw a large dark shape swimming menacingly towards him.

He bolted.

He was too far out to sea to swim back to the ice which he had left earlier, so he swam east towards what he hoped would be a safe place. Looking back he saw that his worst fears had come true. He was being pursued by a Leopard Seal. The Leopard Seal was gaining on him. He noticed a wall of ice and sped towards it. As he got closer to the ice wall he spied a small opening tiny enough to let him in but not the Leopard Seal.

He zoomed towards it.

He only just made it.

Another quarter of a second and the Leopard Seal would have clamped its jaws shut right on the Emperor Penguin's tail.

The Leopard Seal crashed into the ice and the whole wall shuddered with the force of it. Then it swam away, defeated. Even then the Emperor Penguin stayed as long as his lungs could bear in the opening until he could no longer see the Leopard Seal. Then he emerged and darted towards the surface for air.

After he felt his heart stop racing he started to think about his stomach again. There were no fish in this part of the ocean so he began to head in the direction of home, even though it was just over a mile away, now he had been chased away from it.

When he had almost reached the safe haven of his home a black and white figure loomed up behind him. He realised he was in shadow and turned around. A humongous Killer Whale was close behind him. He started charging towards the mainland at lightning speed. The Killer Whale followed him. He was about fifty metres away from the ice and the Killer Whale was close behind. He leapt onto the ice and narrowly missed getting hit by the whale when it ran aground on the ice.

Underneath the Killer Whale the ice started to crack. It groaned and creaked and shuddered.

Finally as the terrified penguin looked on, it collapsed with the weight, releasing the massive creature back into the waiting sea.

***

After all that excitement and being chased the Emperor Penguin slowly started the journey back home with a half-full tummy, but he wasn't going to take any more risks today.

About the author

Daniel Maltz is a 10 year old Nintendo (Mario) fanatic who lives with his mum, dad and younger sister. He lives in Northwood and goes to school at St.Martins. He spends most of his time absorbed in his 3DS. He chose a penguin for his story because he loves (!!!!!) penguins and thinks they are very cute.

To be honest, he doesn't think he really enjoys writing, but his English teacher is very persuasive and managed to get him to submit his story. When he found out his story was going to be published, he was amazed! He couldn't wait for it to come out!

There are quite a few interesting/strange things about him but the main one is that he was once hit by a van outside his school. He broke his tibia and his fibula. He also has type 1 diabetes which is a pain but doesn't stop him doing stuff.

Hannah Probyn-Duncan

Spirit

The warm salty water of the big big blue washed over my body as I dived through the tickly wet seaweed, chasing the floppy white jellyfish and scaring the tiny blue and red crabs. The sunlight flickered and danced on the sea floor as I played hide and seek with a big catfish.

When we both got bored he swam away and I nosed in the sand for shells and shrimps. Then I saw my mummy and my two shy brothers coming and I swam as fast as I could to meet them.

That evening as the sky darkened I followed my mum through the rocks and out into the wide, wide sea, and as I snuggled close to her warm wet side I knew I'd always be safe with my pod. As the sun crept over the horizon me and my friends went to jump the rocks and catch fish near the Hawaiian shore where we lived. We played and played jumping and splashing, diving and chasing each other round and round. And as we were playing an enormous dark shape loomed into my sight; I clicked and squealed to warn the others, and then at top speed I bolted off and managed to dodge the jaws of a hungry killer whale. But not all the young calves were as lucky as me and one of my best friends was killed.

All that night I mourned and cried and my heart ached

and wrenched with such bitterness I could not rest. In the morning my friends managed to cheer me up by helping me stalk a reef shark and jumping through the waves of the big boats. We had such fun and on one of the boats some children and their parents pointed at us and shouted "Dolphins! Oh! Little baby ones... look!"

As we were all swimming back to the pod I looked up and saw that the sky was black, and just as I reached my mum a shaky white hand of light split the sky. Then there was a crash and the biggest wave I had ever seen rose up like a wall of water. Staying as close to my mum as I could I dived through the dark churning waters. Just then I saw a really big jellyfish, and forgetting the storm I chased it.

When it disappeared I turned to find that my pod was gone. I was alone in the wild sea.

I cried for help but the only answer I heard was the crash of the thunder and the terrible roar of the sea as the wind whipped it into a foaming monster. I stuck my head out into the chaos and breathed the damp air, but I was facing the wrong way and I didn't see the wave that rose silently behind me and when I turned it was too late, the wave caught me and I was thrown through the foaming, bubbling depths. I saw the shape of a rock in front of me and I tried to dodge it, but the force of the water was too strong and it smashed me into the rock. Instantly the whole world changed, when I opened my eyes all I could see was whirling white and blue spirals.

Everything seemed to sound muffled and distant and when I shut my eyes it felt like my head was spinning. I felt so dizzy and weak I only had the strength left to lift my shaky head out of the water and breathe. And after that I don't remember anything. I think I must have just been tossed about half unconscious the rest of the night, for when I opened my eyes the sun was shining. I looked around. I didn't even know if I was still in the Pacific Ocean any more.

For the rest of the day I followed boats and caught big fish from the enormous shoals that swam helter-skelter through the yellowish-brown seaweed. I spent many days in this way until one day I saw the biggest shoal of fish I had ever seen. I swam towards them and feasted on them, but as I was about to leave I realised that I was tangled up in a thick net of rope. I tried to wrench free but I only gashed my sides making them bleed. Just as I was about to give up hope of ever getting away, the net was pulled out of the water and the fish were taken out. I shakily looked up to see the deep, kind eyes set in the old wrinkled, weather-beaten face of an old fisherman.

He beckoned to some younger men who came over and stood around me, smiling warmly. Then they got to work untangling me from their net, they also bathed my wounds, stroking me and speaking to me softly all the time, and then gently they lowered me down into the water. With much joy I leapt away from the boat, jumping and splashing merrily. As I dived down into the water I saw a whole cluster of dark shapes swimming towards me. And

just as I was about to dash away I realised it was my own beloved pod. For the rest of the day I played and danced with the calves and knew that I was safe again at last.

'Dolphin' by Charlotte Ash

About the author

Hannah Rose Probyn-Duncan attends Ringwood Waldorf School and lives in the New Forest, with her mum, dad, her three gerbils, Midnight, Sillky and Benji, her cat, Phoebe, 12 fish and a shrimp!

She loves animals, art and story-writing and she supports Wolf Trust and WDCS and adopts a dolphin called Rainbow and whale called Reflection.

Having her story published is one of the most exciting things in her life! Hannah thinks that all wild animals deserve to be free. She has rescued many injured animals, including an owl, a baby rook, a swallow, a baby house martin, a dove, a pigeon, a blue tit, a hedgehog and a baby squirrel, and has even stroked a wolf, called Duma!

Her story is dedicated to Sillky, her beloved rabbit who passed away, and to Serena, the tawny owl who she helped back into the wild.

Drawing by the author, Hannah Probyn-Duncan

Years 7 and 8

A note from our judge, Lauren St.John

Lauren St John was born in Gatooma, Rhodesia, now Kadoma, Zimbabwe. At the age of eleven she and her family moved to Rainbow's End farm in Gadzema, which later became the subject of her memoir, *Rainbow's End*. After studying journalism in Harare, she relocated to England, where she was for nearly a decade golf correspondent to *The Sunday Times*. She is the author of several books on sports and music, including *Hardcore Troubadour: The Life & Near Death of Steve Earle*; and the multi award-winning children's series, *The White Giraffe, Dolphin Song, The Last Leopard* and *The Elephant's Tale*. *Dead Man's Cove*, the first in her mystery series featuring 11-year-old detective, Laura Marlin, who lives in St Ives, Cornwall, won the 2011 Blue Peter Book of the Year Award and was shortlisted for Children's Book of the Year at the Galaxy National Book Awards. Her latest novel, *The One Dollar Horse* was released on 1 March 2012.

As a Born Free Foundation ambassador, Lauren was thrilled to be asked to be one of the judges.

"The shortlisted stories are wonderful. The standard is incredibly high. It was tough choosing the best ones, but at the same time the winners have done something quite special. For me, the winning story is Ella Cantó - she sang. It's a deeply

moving story, written with tremendous skill and sensitivity. It has both power and grace, a potent combination. The runner up is The Crossing another beautifully written story, which shows great empathy for the plight of the migrating wildebeest. It's a wonderful achievement. Two others that deserve special mention are A Lemur's Tale and Hyena's Magic."

Winning Story Years 7 and 8

Marged Enlli Shakespear Huws
Ella Cantó – she sang

I breathed heavily, sucking the salty, fresh air.

The sun bathed my face, and the small scattered salt and water drops on my sun glasses reflected star-like patterns on the shaded hull, smudging my view of what the Cape Verdean mountains washed their feet in. It was obvious that those dry monsters were having a beating from the wind, because the whistling in my ears was quite insufferable as I pulled and heaved, pulled and heaved, pulled and heaved the small, colourful and stripy fishing rowing boat towards the shore.

Like today, a broad smile was stamped on my face. I seem to remember being happy, happy to be out of the clutches of the pair of grumpy and half-witted beasts, which were my aunts. I knew nothing of her existence, especially at that moment, as I peered around at the beautiful turquoise, gigantic pond. She swam into my life elegantly. Within her, she held dignity, great power and wisdom which didn't always show through her shining innocence and harmlessness.

It's strange to say that I once loved a sea turtle. It's certainly a strange way of describing the relationship, but she changed me. She reminded me of my sister and somehow I loved her for what she did.

I reached the shore, trying hard not to think of going home – the large incredibly white house I was supposed to call home, but I had failed to do so since arriving there three months before my first encounter with Tabita.

I pulled the knot, which hung heavily on an old, sinking, badly eroded post tight, making perfectly sure that the boat didn't float away overnight. Running quickly along the beach I was about to turn on to a path when I decided to stop. I don't understand to this day why I stopped, but I did. Turning back around to face the waves, I sat down. The sun shone as I just sat quietly still, a mere silhouette on the beach as the sun descended in the sky. Samba was right, the sky was spectacular; bright colours were being thrown carelessly by an eccentric painter. The island glowed orange, hot red and gold; a pirate's treasure, hidden from the world and only revealing its magnificence at sunset, like a baby lost in the great sea.

I was transfixed by the sight, amazed as when I first visited a gallery. I decided I would return every night. Looking up I saw the Lion Mountain; the perfect place for the perfect view.

It suddenly became dark and cold. Goose bumps spread fast like running water along my arms and legs. Pulling hard on my hoody I rocked backwards and forwards, whistling and humming, trying to reassure myself as the night closed about me. My eyes became accustomed to the darkness. I watched the waves draw nearer and nearer. I didn't flinch. I was perfectly calm. Like a predator catching its first glimpse of its lunch, I froze.

A black unidentified wave-gliding object was advancing closer and closer. I stood up and walked forwards. Then

I sat on a rock at the edge of the water. Closer it came – I watched, not moving. Closer it came – I gasped. Closer it came – I smiled. The U.W.O was a turtle.

She dragged her body hurriedly, leaving a long trail behind her, the half-moons of her flippers on each side. She rushed up the beach and I followed her up, stepping cautiously. She flopped down, tired with all the effort. She began to dig, throwing sand and shells in all directions. That's when I noticed the white material sticking out of her mouth. Breathing heavily she made a distressing sound like a broken air conditioner. It was obvious the material wasn't doing her any good. The sound became louder and she looked around helplessly. I realised what she'd done.

The Marine Biology department back at Bangor University used to campaign about turtles mistaking plastic bags for jelly fish – which can result in death!

She couldn't throw up. I felt hot, sweat rolled like waves down my skin. I didn't have time to think. I tugged on the plastic, knowing quite well that she could bite me or that I could pull her insides out. Both of us were there wrestling with it, trying hard not to hurt one another. It came out all in one go. Luckily, she'd only started to eat her dangerous meal and most of it was still in her mouth. I held it up and we both inspected the wet, draping piece of plastic.

She kicked a shell into my face, reminding me of her business. She was one determined turtle. To make her comfortable in my presence, I walked steadily some metres away. She took her time before parking neatly and laying. Yes, she laid about a hundred eggs after that experience, in order for one turtle from that nest to make it to adulthood and come back to that beach twenty years later. She covered the nest and then made shallow dips around it as a trick and started on her way back. I inspected her rusty colour, massive head and strong jaws: an obvious Loggerhead.

The hotel lights shone down on her and they sparkled like fireworks in her eyes, damaging her eyesight in a magical show. Just before she took off I noted her tag number. She managed to cruise on the waves in an elegant manner. She left just like that.

Briskly I ran on towards a lonely shack.

***

A pleased large smile greeted me. Boro, Samba's son was waiting outside a small, driftwood shack. "Boro, b-oa-t is-s on th-e be-each." I pointed in an effort to break the blank expression on Boro's face. Eventually he smiled and gave the thumbs-up. After disappearing he reappeared with a piece of turtle shaped carved driftwood. We exchanged similar trinkets which I've kept, reminding me of my childhood. Thanking him, I mentioned the beautiful sky and the turtle. He replied with Tabita. It's echoed in my mind ever since.

Later at home my aunts didn't notice me nor the waterfall of sand from the balcony! I went to bed, dreams brewing in my head like a stew.

Samba woke me early to leave for the market. Seeing the colours reminded me of the sunset, smelling the spices and fish – the salty air and whistling of the luggage carrier – the wind in my ears. The word *Tabita* caught my eye again. Samba followed my gaze.

"Tabita means elegance. Also it's a person's name. In my hand is a turtle caller the poachers used to use. Blow through it and the gliding queen will come and sing back to you."

Though puzzling, I learned a lot from him especially about turtles. Perched on Lion Mountain I painted, wrote and read for days on end, watching the ever changing sky and sea, increasing my interest in turtles. I imagined being a turtle, being eaten by crabs when young, and in turn eating them when older; being one of the earth's most ancient creatures and living over eighty years. I would navigate around the world meeting different obstacles and survive especially human threats. How and where was Tabita now? I could only imagine. But was she safe?

***

I came across her again. One evening, I arrived late on the beach after carving a turtle-caller with Boro. I had learned that she would come again about now, fifty days later, to lay again. There was a strange atmosphere which made my mind wander. Thoughts that I usually dismissed about the past, the present and the raging future whirled in my mind. After finding myself standing on the edge of the water I reached into my pocket. My fingers were cold and sore after the effort of carving the caller. Everything was quiet and still, brewing like before a storm. This triggered emotions inside me. Like lashing rain a wave of tears swept over me.

My sister would have loved it here. The last I saw of her was when we walked along Newborough Beach. We had talked all the way to the island. Stars had twinkled as she reassured me that whatever would happen next she would be there by my side, palm in palm. These untrue words had fallen broken on her lips.

Gritting my teeth I washed tears away, after blowing

the caller and waited for the echoing cliffs to deliver. Looking back, I really was waiting for my sister, but something did emerge. Dark and heavy but elegant as ever, she reached

Drawing by the author, Marged Enlli Shakespear Huws

me and in my mind I heard her. She sang on and on, an unheard melody, only ringing in my mind, raising the roof in a triumphant, imaginary performance.

I smiled, laughed and cried. At that moment I named her Tabita and as I let go of my sister, ella cantó siempre – she sang on.

About the author

Marged Enlli Shakespear Huws comes from a small village called Pentir outside Bangor, North Wales. She travels on the bus every day to Ysgol Tryfan, a Welsh medium school in the second smallest city in Britain, Bangor.

She loves all the arts in general including drawing and painting art, music, drama and writing. She has always loved animals and hopes to be a conservation vet when she's older. In the summer she visited Cape Verde that sowed the seed for the story. Whilst there she met the S.O.S Cape Verde Turtles conservation group, and wanting to know more, she ventured on a night-watch with them. She learned a lot about the problems and obstacles the turtles have to face whilst returning to their birthplace to lay their eggs, and even came across a crate full of poacher's tools.

After meeting a turtle she put pen to paper and wrote the story.

She would like to dedicate the story to the S.O.S Cape Verde Turtles group for their hard work. Being published has given her an ambition to keep going despite recently discovering she has a mild learning difficulty, and to become an author after becoming a vet.

Runner-up

Kabir Mann

The Crossing

I looked around; I saw no-one. The emerald grass whipped at my hooves, stirring in the lukewarm breeze. I was rotating around in search of my wildebeest brothers, but I detected no signs of movement. Close by an isolated tree, with writhing boughs curled into its trunk, outstretched its frail olive fingers, all of them pointing out behind me. I turned and focused my cinnamon eyes upon the expanse in the distance.

It was the migrating season. The herd had crossed the Serengeti, departing in an attempt to reach the more luscious grasses beyond, but I was left behind. I had to reach the herd before it was too late as I knew only too well what happened to stragglers left alone in the ominous expanse of the savannah. I trotted through the grassland, the mud squelching beneath my feet, crushing the grass that met the base of my hooves. To the left, in a low ditch, I saw a flayed wildebeest corpse, the brown roughened skin shredded into red and white.

My breath snorted heavily as my pace quickened. To my immediate left the grasses stirred and through the gap two hyenas stared blankly, opened their jaws and then disappeared. A whoop and cry echoed to my right and I jerked my head in the direction of the noise, lowering my horns in readiness. Nothing could be seen, but the tall grasses stirred more heavily than the wind should have allowed. They were trying to surround me. As a seasoned wildebeest of a dozen years, I knew that I had to increase my momentum as then even two or three of the dogs would struggle to pull me down.

I did not know how long I ran, only that when I suddenly stopped, my sides were slick, dust caked my fur and my breath came in heavy snorts. What stopped me was the sudden vision of the Serengeti River clearing through the midday haze. I turned on my hooves and looked back for signs of the slack-jawed mongrels, but the savannah was still. I squinted along the grassy stalks. I sniffed the air. There was time enough to cross the river. Turning, I trotted down the incline to the river bank. Silence hung heavily in the air, deep and oppressive. The tranquil sapphire water of the river glistened like a thousand stars, reflecting the blazing orb in the pillow-stained sky. I stared intently into the deep water of the river as memories of previous crossings with the herd came back to me. The panicked rush, the sudden white surge, a drifting wildebeest held fast by something that pulls it across and then down into the waters. I looked at the sapphire colour and remembered how easily it transformed into red.

The hairs on my muscular neck stood upwards. I turned on my hooves and watched the grasses again; nothing. Turning back to the river I realised that in previous crossings, the herd provided safety in numbers. But this would not be the case this time. I hoped that whatever stalked previous migrations would not be aware that I had separated from the herd; that I was late.

A white bird drifted down onto the water in front of me, gently flapping its wings, as if it had not a care in the world. Or maybe it was too small to bother with? Was it a taunt, a trick? I pricked my ears and fixed my beady eyes upon the surface of the river. The glassy channel stared back at me, motionless. I noticed the imprints of hooves on the other bank – my brothers calling me on. I then heard whooping behind me. Snorting, I dipped my hoof into the water, shook my horns and made ready to take the plunge. But then, by a rock on the far side, I spotted ruts and stains of blood imprinted in the soil. There had been some casualties, yet the corpses were not visible. I plunged into the water, casting ripples to the edges of the river, as I made for the far side.

My eyes darted from side to side.

All was still.

Nothing moved, except for my thrashing hooves. Eyes fixed on the hoof prints on the far bank, I ploughed through the water. I twisted my head to the left and saw the white bird suddenly fly away, squawking wildly.

Was it a signal or a warning? Why could I now not hear the yelping mongrels?

The far bank was now very close. But so too was the vision of the bloody ruts in the mud. I turned my head to look behind me, and just as my hooves began to clatter on the river bed, I noticed a long grey rock just above the water line glide noiselessly toward me. My heart skipped a beat but my hooves trampled vigorously forward, my neck and shoulders rising out of the water as I neared the bank. I then heard the rush of water behind me, the same surging noise of previous river crossings, but this time much louder, more personal. The grey rock must be a mountain behind me. But with one last heave I clambered up the river bank.

It was a few moments before I cantered around to look behind me.

The river was still. It remained blue, not red.

And across the river, cowering on their hind legs, the three hyenas watched in wide eyed silence. I had escaped the grey rock, but they had seen it.

About the author

Kabir Mann is a 13-year-old schoolboy of Haberdashers' Aske's Boys' School and lives with his mum, dad and older brother in London. In Kabir's story, the lone Wildebeest struggling to rejoin the herd is a metaphor of Nature's fight against the challenges posed by Man. Kabir certainly hopes that Nature, like the Wildebeest, will survive. He considers it a privilege to be published in the first Paws n Claws edition and to support the Born Free Foundation.

Kabir has a strong interest in magic, sport and adventure stories.

He has dedicated his story to his family.

Highly Commended

Eve Taggart

A Lemur's Tale

With a leap, I scamper up the trunk of the tree.

The fossa that has been threatening to tear me to pieces shoots up after me and sits hungrily behind, orange light reflecting off its eyes. I do a secret little smile and bound through the branches. Trees surround me as far as I can see. It's been like this ever since I was born, snakes and fossas trying to eat me, but I've always survived.

I dart through the trees, more than I can possibly count, at full speed. The fossa chases me, close on my ringed tail at all times. After so many years of escaping, I've come to enjoy the little game they play with me. I know that someday I will be caught, but I see no harm in having fun while I still live to tell my tale. My tail automatically curls round a branch above me and grasps it. I'm sent sailing into the air, almost elegant in my flying escape. The fossa is unable to follow as the gap is too big, and stays sat on the tree I just departed from, looking very angry. No dinner tonight, silly fossa.

My tail helps me as I swoop like a bird through the trees. I'm showing off to no-one, but I have fun dropping what seems like miles and saving myself from certain death at the last second using it. Suddenly the fossa appears and jumps at me while I'm hanging, stalking me on the ground now. I wrench myself up in terror. I am no longer thinking of this as a game: showing off is, after all, how my mother died. My father, I believe, was caught and taken to a place called a Pete's Pets. No-one in my family knows what it is, but old Aunt Rindra was able to, with difficulty, read the side of the thing that stole him away.

Suddenly a wiry item that looks somewhat like a blanket drops. I'm knocked off my branch and caught in it as I fall. While I hang I glance round for the fossa, and see it in a similar looking thing nearby. We're both suspended from an enormous metal contraption with spinning flat poles on the top of it. A voice floats down from high above me. I struggle onto my feet and strain to hear.

"We've caught you a lemur and a fossa, boss!"

The next person to speak doesn't sound nice. His voice grins at me with pointed teeth. "Well done. Lemurs should get on well with humans. Perhaps not the fossa, but we'll see!"

As we float away, the forest I've known for my whole life is left behind me. I can't believe someone would do this: replace the known and loved life of an average lemur with a new one. As my life is left behind me, I realise that I will very, very soon know what the Pete's Pets thing that took away my father really is. That soon is too soon for me.

About the author

Eve Taggart is 13-years-old and lives in Northern Ireland with her parents, sister and cat Willow. She enjoys writing because she likes creating worlds and characters to live in them. Eve chose a lemur because she has always loved them, for as long as she can remember. She likes playing guitar and her favourite author is Derek Landy.

She wants to be a doctor, and dedicates her story to the memory of her Great-Gran and Great-Grandad, and of Binka the cat who lived with her before Willow.

Paws for Thought Discussion Point

Stories should whet our appetites to want to learn; to find out more about the animals in the stories. Do you know what a fossa is? Why not see what you can find out about it, and how it lives. Maybe you also want to find out more about the Ring-Tailed Lemur. Take a look at the fabulous drawing of one.

'Ring-Tailed Lemur' by Morgan Joy Ashby

Highly Commended

Imogen Hartmann

Hyena's Magic

The sun hadn't yet risen when Mum shook me and Anna, my younger sister, awake. I didn't mind getting up so early on holiday; you see much better wildlife in the morning.

I stepped out of the wooden chalet and pulled my trainers on, carefully checking for bugs. It was surprisingly cold, considering it was South Africa, but that thought was gone when I looked up. I found myself staring into the deep, soulful eyes of a bush baby. It stared back for a second, head cocked to one side, before scampering off with its fluffy tail bouncing behind it.

I nudged Anna and pointed after it. "Amazing, isn't it?" I whispered.

"Yes, lovely," she replied, "but not magical. I want to see real magic today."

***

The Land Rover thumped and jiggled as it bounced across the African savannah, brushing past white acacia thorns. We had set off for the second time that day, after having some lunch. We didn't see much in the morning, so we were hoping to make up for it now. After a while we saw the unmistakeable silhouette of a long necked giraffe. As people snapped photographs, the game ranger told us how trees can warn each other that a giraffe was coming, using special chemicals that float through the air and then defend themselves by making their leaves taste bitter. "Impossible!" scoffed a few of the other passengers, but the ranger just smiled, a little smugly. I believed him. Nature is full of marvellous talents.

"Wow, that's weird isn't it Anna!" Mum said, her eyes huge with wonder. Mum loves nature almost as much as I do.

Anna nodded slowly. "Bizarre, but not real magic."

***

Drawing by Khairun-Nisaa Ahmed

A while later we were fortunate enough to see a majestic Lilac Breasted Roller, a beautiful bird with a soft purple chest, azure wingtips and golden head. It perched on a tree for a while, studying us closely, before flying off like a rainbow comet. "That's the most beautiful bird in the world," I breathed, watching it soar away.

"It's gorgeous," Anna replied, craning her neck to catch a final glimpse, "wonderful. But not real magic. That's what I want to see the most. *Real magic.*"

***

Darkness was finally drawing in. The truck trundled round, and we began to head back to the camp. Anna still hadn't seen what she called "real magic" but I didn't think it really existed. We were looking at animals, not magicians.

Nothing happened for a while, but then a strange noise pierced the night. The game ranger turned off the main track, following the sound, and we soon saw the bright eyes of a pack of hyenas. They were making an eerie, spine chilling noise that sent electric sparks up and down my spine. It wasn't a bark, or a howl, or a growl.

It was singing, an otherworldly, canine singing, as though the hyenas were serenading the moon. I glanced at Anna, who looked at me, and grinned. "That's real magic."

About the author

Imogen Hartmann lives in Ealing with her granny, her parents and her rather idiosyncratic cat. She loves writing stories and poems as she enjoys unleashing her vivid imagination on innocent readers. She used to live in South Africa, and all the animal experiences she wrote about in her story she has experienced herself. She picked hyenas in particular because she thinks they are majestic, even if they scavenge for food.

Imogen believes animals have a right to their own space to be wild and roam free. She is very pleased to be published because she wants to be an author when she grows up, particularly writing poems, fantasy novels and short stories.

About the artist

Khairun-Nisaa Ahmed is in her final year at Manor High School in the East Midlands. She first became interested in writing through the English Literature lessons in school. Since then she has created a great many characters who have gone on many quests and she is hopeful that she will become a published author one day. She aspires to be like the characters that she writes about and would like to travel to lots of different countries, including Africa. As a future career she either wants to study to become a vet or a palaeontologist.

She is looking forward to the new academic year when she starts college (no uniform - yeah). In the meantime, she has taken up lots of hobbies such as collecting sea glass, seashells and even unusual shaped pebbles which she keeps in a vanity case that she and her mother decorated with memorable knick-knacks, so they all have a story behind them.

At the moment she is working on Shoujo Art Studio to create her own Manga comics. She can't wait until the holidays because her mother has promised to take her on a beach holiday.

Finally, she hopes to write more stories and draw more pictures for Paws n Claws in the future.

Laura Baliman

George

George trundled happily through the valley. He could see the Western Cwm in the distance. The sunset over it was magnificent but George knew all too well that he should bed down sometime soon, as the nights are very cold in the Himalayas. You see, George was a Nepalese Wildcat.

He spent most of his days strolling along, marvelling at the beauty of the mountains. He was always alone, and wary of the humans with big red jackets, climbing up the mountains. George had got lost when he was six months old, because of a storm. He used to live with his family in the bottom of the valley, near the human town of Pangboche. They were hunting, and George's father Jon was teaching him to creep and crawl.

The rain started to pitter patter, then all of a sudden hell broke loose, and George woke up under a rock, far from his home. George was at first scared, but after a while he rather enjoyed the loneliness and isolation of being solitary with nature.

***

George was a respectable wildcat. He had decent views and philosophies of the world. But on the other hand, he had one setback: arrogance. Although he thought nature was omnipotent, he thought he was rather handsome (I guess he was slightly), rather supreme and godlike and he thought he could get his way all the time, whatever he wanted. He never wanted much but the love of nature; he got this and other things, just by coincidence! This led him to believe he was exclusive or special otherwise he would never be this lucky.

He used to hunt by luck; hiding in hedges and pouncing out when he saw something. If he didn't catch it he got a bit worried, I mean someone who is supreme should not miss a catch!

But this feeling soon left as he came by another kill.

***

The other animals didn't really make friends with George, as he always looked down on them as lower-class. George thought all animals should know that he was purely the highest ranking animal in, well, the area I guess. George had yet to meet humans, of which some felt the same way.

***

One day, in mid-May, typical climbing season, George was being somewhat wary on his travels. He was incredibly ravenous, as he had been fairly lost in the past few weeks. As he climbed up a pinnacle of rock to look around, he saw a high hill, maybe even a mountain that he had not seen before. But there was something different about this hill. Trees grew all around it, filled with luscious fruits and appetising birds.

Then he saw another hill beyond it, the one with the green hut with a spinning thing on the top of it. George knew that hill! That hill was notorious for very unpredictable weather. Exceptionally unpredictable weather.

George had got lost near this hill, and never ventured back.

He knew that if he climbed the hill full of trees he would find food, exquisite, gorgeous food. But then again, he would almost certainly die. George did not think for long, because, as you remember, he was arrogant. He thought that nature would never strike on him, as he was so special. This would be the biggest mistake made by George in his whole lifetime.

So George rushed to the foot of the hill. He was unaware of the thunderous clouds over the horizon, heading his way. He leapt, bounced, hopped and sprang his way up the rock-strewn hill. He never took his eyes off the fruit. But soon enough the birds stopped singing, and the clouds advanced to over George's head. The rain started to drench George. He was freezing; he began to not feel his feet. He climbed into a tiny bivouac and tried to rest.

He had bad, bad dreams of flying; flying above the earth. He had long wings and he flew quickly and smoothly. He was above the clouds and could see the world below. The children were playing, and looked up. "Zombie cat! Zombie cat!" In his dream he felt dead or half-dead maybe. Then he woke up with a start. It was icy cold, and bitter winds blustered around him. But he wanted that fruit so much. He still thought he was supreme, and he would be okay, but this was getting a bit vague in his mind. He forced his way through, but it just wasn't enough.

It seemed George wasn't so special.

He tumbled and tumbled, falling through the hail and wind.

Whoosh, whoosh, crash, crash! BANG.

About the author

Laura Baliman loves animals, especially horses. She would love to be a writer when she grows up but is also interested in animal-related things. Her favourite book is *The Hunger Games*. She loves writing because she thinks you can express yourself more vividly than in any other way. When she starts writing she can't stop and finds it hard to write really short stories!

Her favourite place is Colorado but she has also always wanted to go into space.

This story is dedicated to Chester the pony, as he would jump the world for anyone.

Paws for Thought Discussion Point

It's a shame we don't have a drawing of one of these wonderful Wildcats from Asia, there are several species of wildcat found in and around Nepal and the Himalayas, maybe you could name some of them and find out more? How much of the behaviour of the big cats and these wildcats can you see in your own domestic cats?

Jessica Cooper

Ace of Zebras

Life was simple at first, get up, eat, play, and go to sleep again.

But then again when you're a kid everything seems so simple. You see, nobody told me I was a zorse until I was two years old (or thirteen years old in human years).

Then everything changed.

***

It started with my friends' parents pushing their kids away from me, in case I gave them stripe germs. Then there was the whole you're not a horse, you're a zorse. thing. That made me feel really bad, I mean what's so bad about having your legs being a totally different colour to your body – not to mention the tiger like stripes running down my neck and torso.

"Ace, can you come over here a sec."

That woke me out of my day dream. I got up and walked myself to my friend, Acorn, a chestnut cob.

"What?" I asked pushing my way through a lake of ferns.

"I found us a herd; it's quite big too, perfect for us!"

I could sense Acorn's excitement; we had been trying to find a herd to join for days. Each time they checked us over and accepted Acorn, but not me. In fact they didn't want to be anywhere near a zorse. But every time Acorn would not leave my side, he was a loyal friend.

"Are you sure?" I queried shaking my mane. "All the others didn't like me."

Acorn sighed and pawed the ground continuously. "It's just because herds in England aren't used to zorses like you. Where you come from, where was it – oh yeah Africa, they probably love seeing you."

"Maybe," I replied. "Let's give this herd a shot."

***

"What do you mean he's not a horse, he's just a little different?!" Acorn was backing me up once again.

"A little!" The big black hack horse laughed. "I personally think that stripes and a severe leg discolouration is definitely not a kind of horse I know!"

"Yeah that's because you're too dumb to know what a zorse is," Acorn replied sarcastically. "Who are you anyway?"

Just then two smaller dark brown hack horses came up beside the black horse, glanced at me then at Acorn. "Boss, you looked like you were in trouble do you wants us to remove these two?" one of them said.

"Trouble, when was I ever in trouble? Just telling stripes and his friend here to beat it," the black stallion bellowed. Neighing loudly he rose onto his hind legs pausing for a second, before crashing down hard on the ground, millimetres away from our feet.

"Let that be a lesson to you," the other smaller hack said and then they both walked away.

"The name's Jet, now just remind me," the now angry stallion said, "what did you call me earlier?"

I could see where this was going. I had to act fast.

What to do. You couldn't do much in the New Forest. In Africa you could kick up sand into your opponent's face and then run. Not here.

"Hey Jet! I have a name, it's Ace."

I tried to create a diversion so Acorn could do something, but it was useless, this Jet was way out of our league. Even if we had sand on our side it would be hard.

"Yeah, Ace of what – zebras!"

To him this was hysterical and he burst out laughing. We made our move and bolted through the forest.

It wasn't until dusk until we finally stopped, we were tired out but something told me they would come after us. We kept going again. Slowly our trot turned into a walk and we were totally out of energy.

We had to stop somewhere to rest but everywhere was risky. If we slept somewhere they would find us, we'd be meat.

***

"Ace, I'm getting tired, we're going to have to stop. If I walk any longer my legs will collapse!"

"I agree Acorn, but where?"

"We could try that patch of land with the stables." Acorn tiredly pointed out the small group of stable buildings, the light inside the nearby cottage gleamed as bright as the sun-lit sky illuminating its presence in the darkness.

"They might have humans nearby," I added cautiously.

"But there might also be horses that can help us," Acorn chirruped, already preparing to jump the fence blocking his way.

I also jumped the fence with ease. Then we wearily trotted to the stables.

***

"Boss, what's the news?"

"Don't shout so loud they'll hear us, boneheads."

"Right okay, we'll stop talking. So why are we here?"

"They insulted me and my herd, and that duo are going to pay for their unruly actions!"

"I, I totally agree with you. Jet, Sir, have you located the zeb-heb..."

"Zorse you...."

"Quiet I think I've located them, you see near the shire. Charge on my lead, ready one, two..."

***

When we got there we were met by a white shire horse, his

Drawing of a zorse by the author, Jessica Cooper

body was huge (bigger than both mine and Acorn's) and his hooves were tufted with white hair. He stared us in the eyes, whipping his tail back and forth. I didn't know what this horse was playing at, and even though the troublesome stare was hitting me hard I could see a small shimmer of kindness in him.

"Where'd you fellas come from, there's no other stable for miles!"

"Um we're from the New Forest, well Acorn here is. But I'm from Africa…" I started, but before I could even finish my sentence the old shire was talking again.

"Africa? What are you a zebroid or something?"

I sighed and Acorn rolled his big brown eyes at me. "Zorse," I corrected. (At least he was close.)

"Listen, we're having a slight problem and we're being chased by a group of hack horses…"

"Hack horses y' say. They're a bunch of trouble round 'ere . I'd stay out of their way if I were you."

"Storm who's out there sweetie?" A white and brown pinto horse stood in the doorway gazing at us with amazement; her white mane flying through the night. She was a butterfly, beautiful, slender and graceful all at once.

"Oh a bunch of kids, they're having some trouble with a group of hacks."

Acorn and I looked at each other worriedly; if we weren't hidden soon they would find us.

"Oh well you better come inside you look awfully tired." The pinto led us into a cosy but spacious stable with straw on the floor and a small trough of water beside the far edge.

"Thank you so much, I'm really grateful for this," I

said catching the pinto's eyes for a second.

"Well this is Storm, and I'm Snow."

"Pleased to meet you," I said, before starting a conversation.

Acorn nudged me. "Acorn can't you see I'm talking here." I carried on talking to Snow.

Acorn nudged me again, harder this time. "What!" I shouted. Giving him the thanks for disturbing me look.

"It's Jet and the other two," he started horrified. "They're charging towards us!"

I neighed and trotted backwards stumbling on the water trough.

"It's them," Acorn warned before allowing Storm to have a closer look.

"Yes you're right," Storm said, shocked. "Three hacks heading straight for us. The one in the centre must be their leader."

"Yes." I panicked prancing round in frenzy. "Big, black, powerful stallion. We have to move if we want to get away from them." I was already heading for the door.

"No!" Snow shouted calmly. I turned round to face her. "If we run they will just catch up, we have to face up to them!"

"You're right," Acorn said. "There's no use in running."

I looked around at each member of the group, my gaze settled on Acorn with his determined look.

"Right, I wasn't given these stripes for nothing. Let's go!" I cheered rising on my back legs.

Acorn smiled. "You really are the ace of horses – and zebras."

With that we all charged out running head-first into the hacks. I had never battled before, and I was worried.

What if we lost? No. I had to block out bad thoughts. I had to keep running. Anyway no matter what happened I had my friends, and for once I was glad to be different. And now galloping into a group of strong horses, I wasn't scared anymore. I smiled.

Acorn was right; I really was the Ace of Zebras!

About the author

Jessica Cooper is a young writer who lives and goes to school in Dorset. She has many pets including bearded dragons and baby fish. She likes writing because it's fun and imaginative, and also wants to be an author in the future. Jess is obsessed with dragons – which take up 99% of her room, but wrote about horses and zorses because she used to go horse-riding and discovered the existence of zorses on the internet. Jess found out about the Born Free Foundation from her support of other conservation charities and believes animals should have the same rights as humans.

Paws for Thought Discussion Point

I urge you to look up the zorse on the internet like Jessica did. Yes they really do exist and zebras crossed with ponies are sometimes called zonies! And like Jessica's drawing they don't always just look like a blend of horse and zebra, with a horse colouring and stripes, some really can have parts of their body just like a horse and some parts just like a zebra, like an odd patchwork. Imagine what might happen if you crossed other animals with one another? Of course in real life only animals of the same species or very closely related species can breed, as is the case with the horse and the zebra. Interestingly the zorse is usually from a male zebra and a female horse and in Africa, where they breed, the zorse (known as a hybrid when from two different types of animal) is resistant to some diseases that would kill the horse. This makes it more rigorous, i.e. better able to survive. But like mules (look up what these are crosses between, horses and ...?) their offspring are infertile, which means they can't breed. So a zorse can only have a horse and a zebra as its parents and not two zorses. They are fascinating, do find out more and see how many other wild animals have been able to form hybrids like this. What are the advantages and disadvantages? And why couldn't a horse breed with a cow? If it did, what would it be called?

Wyedun Knight
Tiarna

When I was in China doing photography, I met a tigress in a secluded area of the Daxinganling forest who I named Tiarna.

I soon knew her very well and often came to photograph her. I used to come almost every day to watch and photograph her. She didn't mind that I was watching her so often. Once she even came and lay at the edge of the hide from which I watched her. She was such a wonderful tiger. It was perfect; she came frequently to the clearing, and I watched without any fear.

She was, as all tigers are, a very wonderful animal. I will always remember how she loved the dried meat I used to give her. She used to give me a longing, hopeful look when she wanted some of it.

Everything was fine until the poachers came.

They were after Tiarna because tigers in China were used for highly sought after medicine. I tried to stop them, but they shot many times at Tiarna. Fortunately she was only slightly wounded and managed to flee.

I was devastated; all the time that I had spent with her was only a memory.

I continued to go back to the clearing, hoping to see Tiarna, but I'd find no trace of her. Finally I had to accept that she had gone and that I would probably never see her again.

***

Many years went by and still there was no sign of her. So I decided to go and look for her. I just didn't know where to start. However, I went to areas in China where tigers were known to live. There was no way I wouldn't recognise her as she had a distinct black spot under her left eye.

The first place I searched was a forest about fifty miles away from the clearing where I used to watch Tiarna. I spent about twenty days there, always looking for any signs of her presence. Though I saw many other tigers, she was not among them. So I moved on to a small strip of forest near the Great Wall of China for I had heard rumours of an injured tigress. Sadly the tigress, although similar to her, was not Tiarna.

***

After that I travelled round the country, stopping for a few days at some of the other forests, still hoping to come across Tiarna but she was nowhere to be found. Then, almost a year later I heard from a friend of a tigress with Tiarna's markings living in the Pagoda Forest. I was excited at this news and made my way speedily to that area. I spent many fruitless weeks looking for her, finding patterns on some trees, the same as she used to make. And then, after almost two months, I caught a glimpse of her hiding in the bushes.

Now, I had not seen her in almost six years, so I didn't want to frighten her off. I remembered that I used to give her some dried meat every few days. I put two pieces of it down at the bottom of a Ying Ke Pine, scattered

84

a few leaves over them and backed away far enough so that I could just see the tree in the distance and waited. Sure enough, after about fifteen minutes, Tiarna emerged from behind the bushes, sniffed at the bottom of the tree where the dried meat was hidden. Then she touched the leaves with her paw, nudged them off the dried meat and started to eat. After that she stood up, looked around, then ambled off towards the stream about two hundred metres away from the Ying Ke Pine.

It was an exhilarating moment for me. After six years of looking for her, I had finally found her so far from where I first met her. I knew I would have to wait before I could show myself to her or even start taking pictures. I memorised where the Ying Ke Pine was and marched triumphantly back to the edge of the forest where I was camping.

Two days later I came back and waited for a few hours. She came at about three in the afternoon. I had put the dried meat down at the same tree before she arrived. Watching her eat it aroused my feelings of fondness for this magnificent creature.

Sadly, on the twelfth day Tiarna spotted me.

From then on she became more cautious. I only sometimes saw her after that. But I was desperate to get her to trust me. Thus, I carried on coming to the Ying Ke Pine, leaving the meat there. Even though it was getting eaten, I didn't see Tiarna anymore.

Then, after a few weeks – there she was again! She was at the stream swimming in the cool spring water. At first I didn't get too close, but soon I crouched down and walked closer to where she was swimming. I put down some strips of meat and hid away. Tiarna came to eat soon after.

I carried on going to the stream where I had seen her swimming, and most of the time found her lying on the banks. She had seen me a few times and wasn't so cautious anymore. She once even came to a few metres away from where I watched her, and let me take a few photos of her. She was becoming more relaxed around me and lying in the sun, almost two metres away from where I was hiding.

She trusted me at last again.

***

Drawing by Charlotte Ash

I came to watch Tiarna many times over the next few years, always taking many photographs. But one day, she didn't come. I went to the stream a few more times, but I knew. Instinctively I knew she was dead.

Tiarna, the most wonderful, amazing animal I had ever had the honour to get to know had died. I had thought of her as being immortal, like a god. I still think of her at times, but I am just happy to have known her when she was alive and to think that she is probably watching over me.

About the author

Wyedun Knight is a 13-year-old boy living in Robertson, South Africa. He likes sport, as well as creative writing. He wants to become an environmental journalist. He has known about and supported Born Free for more than half of his life. He is very concerned about climate change and the extinction of animal species.

He has an environmental blog and has published several articles on it so far.

Wyedun likes to collect and wear caps from various events as well as collecting crystals in and around nature reserves and mountainous areas.

He is qualified in level one of first aid.

Emily Wootton

The Trouble with Skunks

I wake up in the morning with a feeling of dread.

Every day it's the same. I brush my teeth with garlic paste (it's a tradition in my family, and who would be so terrible to ignore tradition?), have a mud bath, (mud is good for the pores, Errol the owl says), then brush my fur with pig bristles. (A pig gave them to my great-grandfather, it is a family heirloom, and it would be rude not to use it.)

After all this preparation, and after I've eaten my breakfast, of course, you would think I had finished getting ready for the day, however, my friends, I must prepare for what is waiting for me outside. Children. Yes, yes, you may laugh. Yes, yes harmless you may think, but I can assure you, no! They are not sweet, innocent widdle corn snakes and wolverine, oh no! They taunt me, tease me! Every morning without fail. I am nocturnal (I have no choice – I wake up in the morning because they wake me), and so is that corn snake. He must really enjoy this sport if he can wake up in the morning.

But anyway, before I get riled up enough to batter them, I reluctantly come out of my abode, smelling so sweetly of garlic may I add, to see them collapsing in a fit of laughter. Even when I don't use my garlic paste, have my mud bath and brush with the pig bristles, they still laugh. Why? I ask myself. Why? I, personally think it is because they are there and laugh to avoid the disappointment that I don't use these things…

"Look at the skunk!" they cry.

"Yeah, Rance, the skunk! Rancid the skunk, more like!"

This is Malico, the beastly little corn snake. His words hurt more than his fangs do, I'm sure. It may not seem that bad, but other things he has spat from his forked tongue are.

"Look at the skunk? Smell the skunk, more like! Ha ha ha!"

This, on the other hand is the wicked wolverine, Brutus. (Or Brutie to me as he is just that: a real brute.) He is dumb and slow, but strong. It's a good job I'm faster than him. He hasn't just got the hang of sprinting yet. With him, it's either stop or slow-mo fortunately.

Yes, every day I am forced to put up with these vile specimens. I must skirt past them whilst they hurl abuse at me. I must enter the forest with them threatening me with death, or worse. Well, I haven't heard them but still, you can guess! But, worst of all, I must live with their words swirling around my (big) brain every second of every minute of every hour of every… you get the picture! I obviously don't exaggerate; these beasts practically ruin my life!

Anyway, when I finally get past them and into the safe sanctuary that is the middle of the forest, I can breathe out a sigh of relief. They wouldn't dare get that close to me now: there are others around. But that's the thing. No one comes within a metre or so of me. I don't know why, I don't have a clue! This is why I am going to ask Errol, the Great Grey Owl, if he can tell me. He is the wisest creature in this whole forest, you know. Surely he will know the answer!

***

I trudge along the forest floor, avoiding the sticks and fallen leaves in vain. It is late autumn, early winter. Suddenly, scurrying along, going in the same direction as me, is my good friend Theo, the tree porcupine!

"Hello Theo!" I call out, hoping to get at least a grunt in response. Theo coughs and inhales. "Oh, er, hello Rance! L-lovely day, isn't it? I must be, uh, off now!" Theo promptly darts up the nearest tree. I sigh, even though I should know better by now.

It isn't long until I see a raven perched on a branch, low down in a tree. It is Riley, and, strange as he is, he never leaves that tree. Never. How he gets food is beyond me, but that's what they say.

"Hey! Riley!" I know my shout has reached him, as I can see him swallow. His eyes widen.

"Riley! Riles?"

Riley wastes no time. I see him jump once. The leaves on the branch shake. I see him jump twice. The leaves fall off, floating down in front of me. Then he squawks raucously and flies off towards the horizon. I don't know where he's gone. I don't even care.

I just know he's gone somewhere away from me.

It seems like hours, days, even, before I reach Errol's tree. The trunk is broad and rotund, and the branches are thick and round, too. There is a gaping oval-shaped hole in the centre.

I'm not that bright, me. I mean, I'm Rance. When I went to be educated my parents called it my teacher-to-be took one look at me and scarpered. Well, he took one whiff of me, I suppose, if Brutie's right. So I don't have the foggiest idea where a Great Grey Owl lives – inside or outside a tree. Anyway, it doesn't matter because Errol's clever.

Whether Great Grey Owls live in a hole-in-a-tree or not, he would not have cared. Errol would have lived in a hole anyway. He's not like a normal Great Grey Owl. He's extremely intelligent, but he hates the cold. Yup, he's clever, that one, living inside a tree instead of out of it because of his likes and dislikes. It's near the bottom of the tree so creatures like me can jump to get inside to

'Fleur' by the author, Emily Wootton

ask him something, but not too low. It just seems great to me because I wouldn't have thought of it. I don't mind the cold.

Before I jump in the hole, questions pop into my head. Am I ugly? Maybe that's why the others can't bear to look at me! Or I'm fat! Yes, I bet that's it! I wish I hadn't come! But I don't give in, and leap as high as I can, and then land inside Errol's home.

He's already awake. His eyes are wide. He looks like he's had a nightmare!

"Oh, hello, Rance…" He welcomes me as if he's in a trance. He swoons, and falls off his perch, near me. As soon as he hits the floor he flies back to his perch. What's so horrible he can't be next to me for more than a second?

"Coo, Rance, forgive me. W-what do you wish to know?" he inhales.

"Well… just like you've done now," Errol looks at me indignantly when I say this, "people avoid me. Why? A-am I fat?"

"W-well, Rance. You are a skunk. You may not know this, as there are no other skunks around and you had no education, skunks… smell. That is the answer to your question."

"Oh… How can I prevent it?"

"Hmmmm… Tell me what you do in the morning."

So I tell him all about the garlic paste and whatnot, but stop as soon as I come to the bit before Malico and Brutus.

"Well, you could stop using the garlic paste and the pig bristles and bathe in water. You cannot stop the smell, however."

I can tell he doesn't want to speak anymore, because of

my smell, so I say thank you and leave.

In the morning, I hear a noise outside. Oh no, not again. Well, perhaps I should spray my stink over them and see how they like it! I race outside. But, instead of Malico and Brutus, I see another skunk! And she's brushing her teeth with garlic paste and she has some pig bristles...! I rush towards her.

"Er, hi, you–"

"Hello!" She stops in mid brush. "Who are you?" I smile, somewhat idiotically, I must admit. "I-I'm Rance."

"Pleased to meet you, Rance. I'm Fleur."

"Nice to meet you too… Hey, did you see a corn snake and a wolverine here at all!"

"Oh, yes. They were laughing and pointing at me; they must have mistaken me for you. So I sprayed them with my lovely scent and they scarpered!"

"Thank you… Fleur. Erm, I didn't know there was another skunk, where are you from?"

"I live with my family, in a glade in the forest. I came here because I had to find my little brother. He ran off, back home, but then I saw unused garlic... Wait, you didn't know there was another skunk? You live on your own? Well, do you want to live with us? This seems out of the blue but…"

"Yes please! If you don't mind, that is."

So, to cut a long story short, I walked off with Fleur.

"Rance, you've been bathing in a mud bath! You smell nice!"

"Thank you! No one's ever said that to me before!"

About the author

Emily Wootton lives in Littlehampton with her mum and dad, and her three cats called Disney, Misty and Brutie. She goes to the Littlehampton Academy. She likes writing because it's putting the ideas in your imagination to a written story! Emily thinks that animals' environments shouldn't be destroyed for more houses etc. and thinks that animals like tigers shouldn't be hunted. When Emily is older she wants to be either a writer or a vet.

She loves chocolate – and received a lot for Christmas which she gratefully scoffed!

She dedicates her story to Chloe, Millie and Hansen, her family's beloved cats who are now playing in heaven.

Paws for Thought Discussion Point

What do you know about skunks apart from the smell? What's the smell for? Why not find out.

Drawing by Charlotte Ash

Amy Leonard

The Elephant's Tusks

It was just another searing hot day at the watering hole. We guzzled down drink for the long walk ahead. Our young stayed close just in case those crocodiles made an appearance. What sounded like a lion's roar went off in the distance but it was continuous and getting closer.

Everyone alert, the herd looked out at the horizon. Loud bangs rang out in the distance. The humongous male elephants started walking away hastily and the herd followed, not wanting to be left behind. My mother stayed at the back pushing all the young forward. Before I knew it we were all running away from this unknown predator. It looked like a metal box with the top cut off and had four circular objects on the sides whirling around fast. The bangs were getting closer and louder. Behind me I heard an elephant fall to the ground. Looking round I saw what elephant was lying down on the ground.

My mum.

The herd didn't stop, but I did.

I turned around and walked towards her. I willed her to get up, pleaded with her. But I knew she couldn't. In the middle of the vast grey of her skin there was red. Blood trickled from her wound. The roar came right up behind me. A click. Silence. I looked at the herd. They were ages away not stopping when one fell behind. Then I looked behind me at the horrors that had killed my mother.

On two legs stood a short animal which had fabric around its body.

A human.

The human didn't scare me. What lay in his hand is what terrified me. It pointed right at me and a feeling told me that this thing lying there was what had done this to my mum.

Two humans came out the back of the truck and cut my mother's beautiful ivory tusks off. One of the humans shouted at the one pointing the lethal weapon at me. Lots of shouting, I stood silently. Another human, clearly furious, came and harshly took the weapon off him. He pushed the man into the metal box. The gun was pointed at me by a different man. His face was unforgiving and his nostrils were flared in anger. Perspiration built on his forehead.

Crack.

His face cracked.

A single tear fell from the corner of his eye. The human broke down in tears and the other humans started crying too. The gun wasn't pointed at me anymore; it lay on the ground by my big, grey feet. He walked over to my mother; put his minuscule hand on her face. Then all of them got into the car and I heard that metallic roar started again.

Whoosh and they were gone.

Just a little blip in the distance. I looked down at my mother.

Never was she going to walk again. Was she going to rot here or would the Hyenas come and finish her off? I stroked my trunk down her grey unmoving face. Night fell like a black cloak and the bright stars twinkled over me. Dawn broke over the African plains. I trumpeted out of my trunk, letting all the animals of the plain understand my sorrow. I saw the herd coming from the distance. They came quickly. A circle was formed around my mum.

Nobody moved.

How could anyone do this to her, take her tusks and leave the rest of her body?

Then one by one we walked on. Leaving her behind. We went towards the blistering morning sun that was dawning on the beautiful African horizon.

About the author

Amy Leonard lives with her mum and brother in Suffolk. She thinks any kind of animal hunting is horrible and would never do it. She enjoys writing and hopes to pursue it as she grows up, but her dream job for the future would be a social worker, as she could help others.

She loves reading and always has a book to hand.

She wants to dedicate this story to all the majestic elephants that roam the world.

Paws for Thought Discussion Point

Check out some of the information on the Born Free website about the ivory trade. Do you think it's right that so many elephants are killed just for an ivory ornament? Something you might like to discuss in class?

Luke Dalby

Mr Hare's Problem

The wild Mr Hare was hopping through the woods one day, he decided to cross a river but the river was too big to hop over.

Mr Hare said to himself, "I know who could help me with this problem, Buck Tooth Beaver".

So Mr Hare hopped over to Buck Tooth Beaver's dam and said to the beaver, "Could you help me cross a big river, Buck Tooth Beaver?" and Beaver replied "Of course I can Mr Hare".

Buck Tooth Beaver and Mr Hare went over to the big

Drawing by Charlotte Ash

river and Buck Tooth said, "This will be easy for me to help you get across."

So Buck Tooth went over to the closest tree to the river and started chopping at it with its razor sharp teeth.

Finally the tree fell down on the ground, and then he used his long, strong tail to push the tree in the water. After that Mr Hare hopped on the edge of the tree and hopped along the tree which was floating in the water. But suddenly Mr Hare had to stop because the tree trunk was too short to go along the river. Mr Hare hopped sadly back to the river bank and to Buck Tooth Beaver.

"Sorry Mr Hare, I thought that would work because it always works for the river I cross," said Buck Tooth Beaver.

"That's alright Buck Tooth do you have any more ideas about crossing the river?" pleaded Mr Hare.

"No, oh wait a minute I do, we could get Elmo the Elephant to help us!" said Buck Tooth Beaver smartly.

"That's a great idea Buck Tooth let's go straight away!" Mr Hare happily said.

They both went towards the water hole where all the elephants hang around. So they searched the water hole to find Elmo the Elephant one of Mr Hare and Buck Tooth Beaver's best friends. Finally Mr Hare and Buck Tooth found Elmo the Elephant and Mr Hare asked her, "Could you help me cross a big river PLEASE?"

Then Elmo the Elephant most kindly said, "You're so polite Mr Hare and you use your manners so well and that's why I'm going to help you."

After that Mr Hare said, "THANK YOU, Elmo the Elephant."

Elmo the Elephant plodded down to the river bank with her friend, to see what she could do.

"I could handle this easily," boastfully said Elmo, she dipped her long trunk into the river and sucked up all of the water. Mr Hare was about to walk across the river bed, but then he heard a big gush of water coming towards him, so Mr Hare quickly hopped back to the river bank.

"Sorry Mr Hare I couldn't hold the water in my trunk for long enough," Elmo said sadly.

"So what shall we do?" they all asked at once.

"You could listen to me!"

Every one turned to see who it was, it was Hoot the Owl that flew in when nobody was looking and landed on a tree.

"Do you have an idea to help us across the river, Hoot?" said Mr Hare.

"Yes I do. You have to work together to achieve your goals. That's why none of your plans worked. This is called team work. By planning together you have more chance of success," plainly said by Hoot

Hoot then just flew away into the sky like nothing ever happened.

Finally they took Hoot's advice and devised a plan which they could do together, they thought of a perfect plan which got everyone excited. First Buck Tooth Beaver cut down two giant oak trees which could easily get across the big river after that Elmo the Elephant pulled the two, big tree trunks to the river bank by using her strong legs; finally Mr Hare put the tree trunks into the water. So Mr Hare, Buck Tooth Beaver and Elmo the Elephant, hopped, walked and plodded to the other side of the river.

And they all said together "IF YOU USE TEAMWORK YOU CAN ACHIEVE ANYTHING."

About the author

Luke Dalby is a 12-year-old boy who lives in Harlow, Essex, with his mum, dad and 16-year-old brother.

He goes to Burnt Mill Academy where he got a task for homework to get something published, so he decided to write an animal story for Paws.

He also enjoys drama and history because he likes to be creative.

His interests in life are horse riding and drama; he also has been in some plays and movies like "Wild Bill" which is coming soon.

Finally he would like to dedicate the story to his mum who helped him by encouraging him to write the story in the first place.

Emma Atkins

The Tale of a Horse

You may think that we horses aren't all that smart – but you're wrong.

We have our own little world that no human knows about. Although all animals have homes of their own, horses have towns and cities. Because we live in a group we all have different roles to play, they are like jobs but we all stay together. Only the leader of the herd and a few other males leave every now and then to search for a new grazing area.

This is a tale about when I went instead.

***

I was only young at the time, barely classed as an adult. I definitely wasn't smart enough to be one. My father was

Drawing by Charlotte Ash

the leader of the herd. He was a proud ruler that in a way inspired me, yet despised me in all that I did. My mother thought the world of him, it wasn't hard to see why, and she wished for me to be a great ruler like him. Back then I loved to mess around and hated the idea of turning out like my father. I just couldn't bear the thought.

I looked nothing like my father, his coat was a fine dark brown and his mane was pure white. While my coat was patchy grey and my mane was scruffy, it was the same colour as my coat yet darker. I don't know how I turned out like this because my mother is chestnut with a brown mane. I think I was found lying out in the cold because my mother had abandoned me, but that's just me.

Anyway, back to my story.

As I said, my father doesn't like me but my mother loves me as much as she loves my father. So one day when one of the grazing land searchers couldn't go my mother suggested that I go. My father hated this idea and so did I, but we knew how happy it would make my mother so he agreed.

My father did all he could to get rid of me and I did the same to him. Unfortunately, the other horses had been told by my mother to keep an eye on me so whenever I wandered off they came and found me. How helpful of them. We travelled a long way until my father finally said, "Come on we better turn back it's getting late."

I stormed ahead mumbling, "I said that ages ago." My father came trotting up to me angrily, "What was that?" he asked. I didn't reply instead I huffed and galloped ahead.

***

I came to a large wood. Although I knew I was going the wrong way I didn't turn back, instead I carried on walking through the dark forest, not knowing where I was going. Suddenly I heard a gun fire, the noise scared me but I stood tall thinking it was nothing. Then I heard another, followed by two more. I reared up, then span round and galloped. I knew I was running for my life.

I finally reached my father. "Hurry, run!" I shouted, "Hunters coming!" My father and the others turned and ran as well. We were heading straight for the herd so I stopped. "We can't lead them to the herd," I told my father, as he stopped beside me.

He nodded in agreement then said, "I have a plan follow me." We all followed him to the cliff, and then he stopped. "Get the others to the top, the hunters' horses won't be able to climb as well as us," my father said, adding, "I'm staying here."

I nodded and escorted the group up the cliff side. When I reached the top I could see everything. Suddenly I saw the hunters. They were headed straight for my father. Just then I forgot how much I hated him and galloped down the cliff to save my father. Many thoughts rushed through my head at that moment but I listened to none of them. I stopped beside my father, "We are doing this together," I said proudly.

As the five hunters lined up in front of us, my father and I got ready. Suddenly we ran through the hunters, knocking them off their horses and on to the ground. I reared up and neighed. As I did this the others came rampaging down the cliff side, kicking any hunters that tried to get back up. The five horses that had belonged to the hunters ran with us, they had become part of the herd.

On that day I finally felt like part of the herd and not just an outsider.

We all galloped at full speed back to the herd. I was in the lead, my father wasn't far behind. "You did well my boy," I heard him say from behind me, "you'll make a fine leader one day."

This made me feel good.

About the author

Emma Atkins is a budding writer who currently spends most of her free time typing away at a computer. She lives in the seaside town of Hastings with her parents, her brother and a lot of pets including: her two cats, Shannon and Joe, her Labrador, Harley, and many fish.

It is these animals that inspire her to write about animals a lot of the time, although another main animal she writes (and draws) about is the horse as she hopes to own one in the future.

Getting published in this book has given Emma a real confidence boast and she hopes to be entering more competitions like this soon. She is also pleased that entering the competition has helped the Born Free the animal charity.

Drawing by the author, Emma Atkins

Years 9-11

A note from our judge, Alan Gibbons

Alan Gibbons has been writing children's books for seventeen years. He is the winner of the Blue Peter Book Award 2000, 'The book I couldn't put down' for his best-selling book *Shadow of the Minotaur*. He was a judge of the 2001 Awards.

He has also been shortlisted for the Carnegie Medal in 2001 and 2003 and twice for the Booktrust Teenage Prize. He has also won the Catalyst Award, the Leicester Book of the Year, the Angus Book of the Year, the Stockport Book Award, the Birmingham Chills Award, the Salford KS4 Award, the Hackney Short Novel Award and the Salford Librarians' Special Award. His books have been published in Japanese, German, Italian, French, Thai, Spanish, Danish, Dutch, Swedish and other languages.

Alan was a teacher for eighteen years, but he is now a full time writer, working with KS1, KS2 and KS3 so has a lot of experience with children's writing.

"It was a tough call as all the stories in this smaller category were strong and could have been selected. In the end I went with 'Stripes' and 'Breaking the Ice' because it had an edge of drama, a fully realised story arc and a real sense of the animal itself. It was a close thing deciding between them."

Winning Story Years 9-11

Jessica Law
Stripes

Stripes burst through the trees and raced along the dusty track.

It was the third time this week that the poachers had found him, and he was getting worried. What would happen to his mate and her young cubs if he was killed? But he had to keep hunting, and that meant he had to keep returning to where the poachers were.

Nervously, Stripes slowed to a steady jog and sniffed the air. It smelt normal – the scent of tree sap dominating the air. Excellent – he had outrun the poachers. He couldn't risk leading them back to where his mate slept with her young cubs – the poachers would kill them all without hesitation. Much more happily, Stripes slipped back into the cover of the forest and jogged over to a small clump of vegetation, before growling softly. A low growl answered his call, and at this point, a pair of warm eyes appeared in front of him – followed by the body of a majestic female tiger.

She was clearly underweight due to the threat of poachers and the strain of caring for cubs, yet there was still an air of majesty about her. Stripes rubbed against her affectionately before heading into the thicker vegetation. Hidden in the undergrowth were the small, sleeping cubs, completely innocent but always under threat. Stripes nudged them gently before turning around and protectively lying beside them. He did his best to protect them from the poachers but he knew that one day they would have to face the world alone.

***

Stripes woke shortly after sunset. This was the time that tigers normally hunted, so it was also the time that the poachers posed the largest threat – however he knew he had to hunt now.

His mate and her cubs needed food urgently. Carefully, Stripes got up and padded softly out of the hiding place. The best food was available about five miles south but many poachers gathered there, so it was safer to hunt in the clearing to the east.

Stripes set off at a steady jog; he had to save his energy in case the poachers saw him while he was hunting. It only took him ten minutes to reach the clearing and he seized the opportunity to hide himself in his favourite spot – behind the oldest tree. If the poachers had been here they would probably have chosen this spot, so it was a good sign that the spot was empty. He didn't have to wait very long for prey – a young wild boar entered the clearing apparently alone. Stripes seized his chance.

He rushed at the boar and grabbed it with his powerful front legs before administering the fatal bite.

Food at last!

Jubilant, Stripes dragged his victim back into the cover of the trees.

***

This single young boar would not last for very long, but it would provide enough nutrition to sustain his mate and cubs for a few days. Stripes started to drag it back to the hiding place. He wouldn't take it all the way as it would leave a trail – just far enough so that his mate didn't have to come out into the open. Once he felt safe he called to his mate, and she soon arrived with the young cubs in tow. It didn't take long for the family to eat all the best bits of the boar, and Stripes knew he had to find another meal while the poachers were away. That way, his family could survive for a while longer. Steadily, he set off again, this time to another good hunting area he knew in the north-east.

That was his mistake.

***

What Stripes didn't know was that the poachers had chosen this area to stake out tonight, and had set some traps in preparation. Almost as soon as Stripes arrived he realised that something was wrong. He turned to leave, before realising that he couldn't – his way was blocked by an absolutely huge vehicle. Suddenly he felt a blow to the back of his head and let out a huge roar, before collapsing to the ground.

He had been caught.

Now he would be killed.

***

Stripes woke up at around midnight. It was pitch black but his excellent vision helped him to realise where he was – he was just outside the forest, not that far from his home! If only he could open the cage he was in he could escape! Quickly, Stripes tried to figure out an escape plan. Soon, he would be transferred from this cage into the transport vehicle. That might be a good time to make a move – but then the poacher might be expecting it then.

Now would be better.

Stripes surveyed his cage. It was incredibly cramped with barely enough room to turn around in – but it was also fairly weak. If he could break the bars then he might be able to slip out. It was time to act. Stripes placed his paws on the bars of his cage and began to push. He shoved the weakest looking bars again and again until finally he heard a creaking sound. The bar was breaking.

With a humungous effort he gave one final shove and the bar snapped off with a large bang. This also had a surprising side effect – the door swung open! With a deafening roar, Stripes leapt out of the tiny cage and raced into the forest.

He was free!

***

Five years later Stripes was lying sleepily beside his mate in the forest. The poachers had left years ago and the forest was a safer place. It was now protected by the government due to the actions of several charities – but Stripes didn't know that. All he knew was that he was now free from the threats of poachers and habitat destruction – free to live a long and happy life surrounded by the family he loved.

About the author

Jess Law lives in rural Wiltshire with her parents, two younger brothers and ten wonderful chickens. She enjoys writing both short and longer stories, reading, hiking and animals.

Her favourite animals are chickens, because they make her laugh, and all types of cats, especially big cats like tigers. Jess supports the Born Free Foundation and is currently adopting a three-legged tiger called Masti. When she is older, she would like to be an author, and to keep both cats and chickens.

This short story was written to help ease post-exam stress, and Jess would like to dedicate it to her wonderful friends and family for their love and support.

Runner-up

Susie Bradley

Breaking the Ice

My first memory is snuggling into my mother's warm, white fur in our underground haven.

Mum and I were blocking out the whirl of the storm above, trying to block out nature, trying to block out the cruelness of nature. She took my sister. Her spirit rested in the corner of our den, a memory of how unfair the world is.

***

That is the first memory of my life, a sad memory of the first few days after I was born. It came flooding to me as I watched my mother disappear over the horizon, a snapshot of the second unfair memory of my life. I was reminded how I might never snuggle against her again.

***

It all happened not long after we had come out of our den. The world was white with a blanket of fresh snow, the same colour as my new coat. The sky was grey with clouds and a brisk wind swept the surface of our kingdom. My mother was starving, having used most of her energy producing milk for me. I wanted to stop and play and dance in the snow, but Mum dragged me down to the sea. It was frozen over but I was still scared as I made my first steps onto the ice. I could hear the sea sloshing as we walked to a piece of ice thin enough to fish from.

The sea was very close – I could see its dark surface from where I was standing. Mum said that any further inland would mean she couldn't bash through the ice. I watched as Mum found a scent that interested her and followed it across the floor. She waited, telling me to stop fidgeting and stay still. Then, feeling the moment was right, she jumped up and down on the ice. The crack hurt my new ears. I ran back, frightened. Mum called me back, cross.

"You shouldn't be scared of ice, you're the King of the Arctic," she said. "Come back!"

I wouldn't move. The ice was still cracking and I didn't like it.

"Come on!" Mum shouted at me.

She came across the ice to get me.

The sound of snapping ice was deafening. Every hair on my body stood on end. It kept on going and going, I thought it would never stop.

That's when it broke away, releasing us into the wild sea.

I howled in horror, turning round, searching for Mum, wanting to hide away. Only to find Mum wasn't with me.

I called and called, silence my only greeting.

This wasn't meant to happen.

The ice is always thick enough, is what Mum said to me, it never cracks.

I trusted Mum. She had been living through Arctic winters for years. So why had it cracked?

Maybe we were too heavy. Maybe…

That's when I heard a roar. I could recognise that sound from miles away. Mum! I roared and roared back, until my throat hurt. She told me how much she loved and missed me and I tried to say it all but I couldn't. And however much we tried, we couldn't get any closer.

I watched until Mum's silhouette disappeared over the horizon. I was alone. What was in the sea? Mum told me nothing could hurt us, but anything could get me. I wanted Mum. I wanted to snuggle up to her in a safe den and forget all about this mess. I want her to protect me, be near me, because no-one else would.

***

I floated on my gradually decreasing ice float for days, the sea my only company. I was hungry and tired, having only caught two dead and sour fish. I was thirsty but the sea water tasted horrible. If my float melted any more there would be no room to stand.

I want Mum.

I repeated this over and over until I fell asleep.

***

A sudden freezing sensation woke me up with a jolt. I took a quick breath of air, but all that filled my lungs was... water!

I opened my eyes, but the water stung them like sour fish in my mouth. Which way was up? Which way was down? I need air. I'm swirling round and round... Where's up? I want air.

Where's my float gone? I want Mum!

My head burst through the surface of the water just in time. I coughed up salty water and replaced it with breaths of cool, clean air. My head disappeared beneath the surface for a second but I was up again. I kicked my legs and found this helped me stay up for longer.

It was only then that I dared open my eyes again. I was surrounded by masses of dark water.

No land. No snow. No ice float.
And still no Mum.

***

I swam like this for what seemed like an eternity. All fears of predators screamed at me constantly. I couldn't sleep or eat. Fear of drowning prevented that. On one paw it was drowning and on the other, it was dying of exhaustion. Unless I found land. Soon.

When I was washed up on the rocky shore of land I'm half drowned, exhausted and starving. I manage to crawl just above the tide line and lie down, ready to die.

***

I am woken by a jolt and the purr of something... not natural, is how I can only describe it as, even now. Around me were bars, endless grey bars. And these bars were in a small space. And driving the space were two humans, although I didn't know this at the time. The cage rocked as we stopped and started, the engine hurt my ears.

Where's the snow? Where's the ice? Where am I?

I look out of the window, a small piece of glass next to me. All I see are houses, the dens humans live in, and chimneys; chimneys churning out dense black smoke. Smoke that pollutes my kingdom and melts ice. Smoke that caused Mum to die and me to nearly. I had given up all hope of Mum surviving the merciless sea.

I was overcome with a surge of anger and began to shake. I bit the bars and rattled the space. I roared and barked to my heart's content. It felt good. I'm in charge. You can't beat me, you animals with roaring machines and black smoke.

The humans shout and stop the car. They get out, open the boot and... Everything goes black.

***

I woke up in a concrete room. It was grey and the floor was covered with straw. Food was in the corner. I rushed over to it and ate hungrily, savouring the flavour. I had eaten nothing for days.

Once I have licked the bowl clean, I explore my new habitat. I find a group of two other young bears. Mum! Mum? No, no Mum. Disappointment engulfed me. I began to cry, letting out all the grief and worry.

"Hey," said a voice. I looked up and found both the bears looking at me inquisitively. "What's wrong?"

I told them my story. They understood.

***

Over the next few weeks I learn from my friends that we are in a place called a zoo. This is a place for animals like me. People come and look at us playing and eating. At first I was shy, but then I learnt to ignore them and live normally. I was happy; at least as happy as I could be, knowing that I will never be free again.

No-one ever found Mum. She probably became a victim of the sea, undiscovered, unknown to all but me. I live the way she would have wanted me to live, happily. I am pregnant with cubs and hope to lead them to a happy and healthy life. I yearn to show them what it is to be free. But I don't know if we ever can be now. This is all we have left. I am only thankful that it is comfortable for us.

My experiences are not unlike many others. Some are lucky. Many are not. This happens because of cars and chimneys and the black smoke that they release into our planet. This happens because of humans.

We need to look after our planet. Or else it won't last us long.

About the author

Susie is 14-years-old and lives in Edinburgh with her mum, dad, sister and brother and their pet gerbils, Pickles and Snuffles. She enjoys skiing and writing because she finds it easier to express her feelings in words on paper and she likes to make up a world that she has complete control of! It means so much to Susie to be published in this book because she has had dreams of being a published writer all her life and this will be the first time she is published but she hopes that there will be many more to follow.

When she is older Susie would like to be a writer or work in the publishing industry, as an editor or agent. Susie enjoys hanging around the house.

This short story is dedicated to her two deceased hamsters, Muffin and Hammie, in memory of all the happy times they had together (and all the times they escaped!).

Paws for Thought Discussion Point

Polar Bears are amazingly beautiful creatures and sadly, as Susie shows in her story, they are losing their habitat; the arctic ice caps are melting. This is attributed to global warming. So the way we treat out planet and reducing our carbon emissions is vital to stop further habitat loss. As the sea-ice melts the ice platforms used by the bears get further and further apart, making swimming more and dangerous and presenting fewer opportunities for hunting. The Polar Bear population is rapidly declining.

Check out the Born Free website to find out more about Polar Bears and think about what you can do to help prevent global warming. How can YOU help make the planet a more eco-friendly place?

Eve Aycock

The Cuckoo Who Cared

I woke up with a start, being jiggled around.

I couldn't fully open my eyes yet; all I saw was darkness. I was enclosed in a thin circular shell, and something was flying, carrying me.

Suddenly, I was dropped, and landed in another warm circle; this one more uneven. My eyes peeled open, and the shell I was in shone tangerine orange, the light of the sunrise shadowing the round shell I was trapped in. I hit the egg hard, breaking it open with my sturdy bill. I saw a big, blue grey stripy bird flying away with wings shaped like sails on yachts, heaving itself into the thickets far away across the jewel green meadow, calling "cuckoo, cuckoo."

In frustration, I had kicked all of the small mud brown eggs out of the swirly, crazy nest made from sickly yellow dried grass that I was stuck in. A small bird with a creamy chest speckled with black swishes with a brown back, and a tiny peachy orange bill and feet, flew up, carrying a plump lime green caterpillar. It leaned over to me as I greedily opened my mouth, and it popped it in my bill. It was the first thing I had ever tasted, and it was good.

Life continued like this, me sitting in the nest while the kind bird flew out extracting beetles, flies, moths and spiders from the green meadow, now dotted with colourful wild flowers as summer grew up. Every day I was growing bigger, and the small meadow pipit seemed to be growing smaller, shrinking. I couldn't believe that this little pipit didn't understand that I wasn't its chick – I looked nothing like it and was practically ten times bigger.

***

Late summer, I learnt to fly.

I enjoyed parachuting through the meadow, watching the flowers die and the leaves turn brown, as if a disease was spreading. And when I got back to the nest, there was always food there for me. One day I heard the soft sound I had heard my real mother sing on the first day of my life. There was a crowd of birds chirping 'cuckoo-cuckoo.'

I had looked up, and seen the same type of birds as me, flying south, for Africa. The meadow pipit – my unofficial mother – was elsewhere, so I had plucked a stripy black barred loose feather from my plumage, as a memento for her. The cuckoos were tiny black dots on the hazy rose pink horizon and I had to fly fast to catch up with them. I was a trifle smaller than them, but I was the fastest flyer. They didn't even notice me joining them, I blended in that well.

We flew as a giant cuckoo crowd, occasionally diving down to catch insects, and then we all rose above the skyline again. The other, older cuckoos told me about Africa; where we were heading. They said the ground was bare, with cracks in the deep orange earth. It was hot, so you had to drink lots of water from the oases that the wrinkly, textured grey animals called elephants played around in, squirting water at each other with long spindly trunks. I could hardly wait to arrive.

***

Eve Aycock

As we arrived in Africa and as time passed by, I drifted apart from the other cuckoos. I learnt how to live the autumn and winter in Africa. I fed on big, juicy beetles from the floor and flew around, enjoying the sunsets that were the colour of burnt honeycomb, with the native animals being silhouetted black against the light. I loved the sunrises in which the sun ran across the lilac lakes, framed with scrawny trees; always a refreshing start to the day.

Soon, it was time to leave Africa. Summer was approaching and it was far too hot to spend the summer in Africa with a full coat of feathers. I had headed back to Britain – I knew the route, and managed to find exactly the same meadow as I was brought up in. The nest I grew up in was gone, demolished, and I was the only bird there in the dark early summer evening, the moon a pale grey ball illuminating the meadow.

***

I spent my days making a circular spiralling nest out of the long blades of grass like the meadow pipit had done for its own chicks, which were only to be knocked out of the nest by me. I was going to raise my own chick, even if I was the first cuckoo ever to do so.

The day came, and the egg was laid. A gem in the land of birds. Who knew a large rock-like egg could hold a living item, which will grow to be as big as me one day? "Cuckoo, cuckoo," I chirped hoarsely, happily. I will protect this egg with my life, I thought. I will fly side by side with the juvenile to Africa. I will teach this chick to fend for itself and carry on the future generation of caring cuckoos; kind enough to look after their own chicks.

About the author

Eve Aycock lives with her family in the Isle of Man. She is interested in art, photography, literature and nature. Eve chose to write about a Cuckoo to raise awareness of the bird, as it is listed as a Red species by the RSPB, which means it needs urgent conservation to save it.

Eve hopes this won't be the last time her work is published, as she would like to pursue a career in law, art, languages or the environment.

Eve based this story on the juvenile Cuckoo she saw last summer when she visited the famous Wildfowl & Wetlands Trust reserve in Slimbridge, Gloucestershire.

Paws for Thought Discussion Point

The cuckoo is what we call a brood parasite; it has adapted to survive by laying its eggs in the nests of other birds and like Eve's cuckoo, the new parent will adopt the bird even though it looks nothing like its other chicks and can grow to be three times larger. In fact the baby cuckoo often pushes the other chicks out of the nest and still the parent feeds it as if her own.

Cuckoos have evolved ways of making their eggs resemble those of the host parent and at the same time host species have adapted ways of being able to recognise the cuckoo's eggs. It's what we call an evolutionary arms race, where nature tries to keep in step, the better the host gets at recognising the eggs, the better the cuckoo gets at disguising them or finding new unsuspecting hosts. Brood parasitism is one of the amazing ways nature has developed for species to survive. Google 'Brood Parasitism' and see how many other birds also use this strategy and see if you can identify ways the host is trying to adapt to prevent it.

Jennifer Llywelyn Jones

Gulliver The Great

"You need to grow up and be more like your sister."

For the billionth time Mum is going on about me not having a family of my own. "You should have a wife and children like your brother."

Oh God, Dad has joined in. My only escape is to run away. I'm the fastest vole around. My family won't bother going after me. Anyway, the only other vole in my family who can fit down my hole is Burt and he can't run yet. Left, right, up, down, tunnel's getting smaller. Up, left, left, up, almost there. Up and out.

Thank God – light!

There are more flowers than I remember. And it's warm. And I can see through the walls. I know – I'll fill in my hole with this rock so they can't follow me. It's very hot in here. And there are big red things. Wonder what they taste like? Emmm taste nice. And small brown things that look tasty too. Eewwwwwww. No don't eat them again.

Thump! What was that? There, the wall at the end of this huge tunnel has opened. I can hear my heart racing! A long thin man has just walked in. It's squeaking. I'm running to that corner behind the big leaf so it won't find me. Don't breathe. It's shouting something like "Oh mattows." It's coming over here. It's got me. It said "Ow din?" It's dark.

I'm gonna die!

We're moving. Save me! Oh no one can hear me. I'm dead! I'm dead!

***

It's taking me away. I can see a bit of light through the cracks. Another thump. We're inside something. It's moving around and there's lots of rustling. Oh it's dropped me! Ha-ha you can't get me. In here I'm safe. You can see me from up there, but you can't reach me. Where am I? It's a box thing. Oh, no air I can't breathe! What kind of torture is this! Pop, pop.

Spikes are coming from the top. Aaaaaaaaaaaa! It's gonna kill me! Mum was right I should have listened save meeee!!!!!!!!!!!!!!

What's that snuffle snort noise? Oh no! A dog! It's gonna kill me! The mans' are gonna feed me to it! "Leev!" The man said something very loud. The dog has gone. Slam! What's that?

Another man, a bigger man is looking at me. It's talking to the one who stole me. "Oo gotta a vole," said the new man. "Yeh. En y geen nouse." What are they saying? I don't want to die! What can I do, I'm trapped. I know, I'll eat my way out; I'll start in the corner where they won't see me. Ewwwwwww. I feel sick! It's not wood. It's not hard paper. It's poison.

I'm gonna die! Why me? I've never hurt them!

Woah! Moving. It's taking me somewhere! It's gonna eat me! Outside? At least I'll see the sky again! It's taken the top away. Why? Is it a trick? I'll pretend to be dead. Nothing's happened. Why would they let me go? Mans are weird. I'll make a dash for it anyway.

I'm free!

No one can hold me prisoner. I outsmarted them with my brilliant charm and good looks. Okay now run. Back door tunnel here I come.

"Mother, Father, Brothers, Sisters I have returned from my adventure." Nobody came to greet me. It was as if I hadn't been away!

"If you do not wish to hear my tale of misery, fine I won't tell you."

Now they look at me. "Oh so you want to know do you? Are you sitting comfortably? No? Oh well, just be quiet and listen!"

"After running away I braved heat and darkness, captivity and torture," the little ones started to wriggle. "Well, it all began when I emerged from my tunnel in a land of milk and honey. It was warm, it was paradise, but only I was to see it, because after I left the tunnel, magic made a rock too heavy for a man to hold and covered the hole. The food was good, life was good. And then it came for me, a two headed monster long, thin and hideous. It had me in its hold and took me to the torture place and put me in the box of poisonous wood. My air ran out and before it let me die it stabbed a big hole in the top only just missing me. And here's the scar to prove it. Then the devil's hound came and swallowed me up at the order of another two headed monster, the one that was bigger and stronger than the first! I chewed my way out of the devil dog's stomach and braved a forest of poisoned ivy to get home to tell you of my adventures. For I am Gulliver the Traveller and Venturer Extraordinaire."

As I wait for applause thwack my mother hits me on

the head.

"What was that for?"

"For telling lies."

***

Two weeks passed and Father came back astonished to say that I didn't lie at all. He said that it had all happened as I had told it, for he had seen the creature but he didn't get caught. After that my name was Gulliver the Great.

About the author

Jennifer Llywelyn Jones is currently studying for GCSEs where she lives with her family in North Wales. Her grandmother Jean Lyon is a published short story writer.

Amongst other things Jennifer writes songs and poetry.

Next year she hopes to attend a local college to study music.

Paws for Thought Discussion Point

Voles are small mouse-like rodents and often you may mistake one for a mouse or even a shrew. Rodents are one of the many wild animals that live close to us as humans; sometimes closer than you might like! Voles can have five to ten litters a year and usually don't live any longer than a year. How many British rodents can you name?

Kristen-Anne Bowen

The Foreigners

My father calls my name, and I gather my hunting weapons. Bow and arrow, spear, dagger. I have everything I need for my first fishing trip. It's an honour, symbolic. It represents my becoming a man. We're headed for the river, my father tells me, and if I catch a fish, we shall eat it tonight.

My uncle tells tales of white skinned outsiders who take down our trees and kill our animals. They speak in a foreign language and wear strange materials on their bodies. They have large weapons made of black metal, and they hurt animals. He says that they only want them for their fur. What kind of person does that? They're such beautiful creatures; they don't do anyone any harm.

***

My father calls my name again, getting impatient and I race outside, bidding farewell to my mother. She is worried about me, scared I will get hurt. I tell her that I'll be okay, that I'm tough, but she does not believe me. She thinks that I am a baby.

We trek through the thick jungle, avoiding snakes and lizards. I have never been this far from my village, and the wildlife is breathtaking. Beautiful parrots sing their songs, if you look closely, you can see a leopard in the distance, monkeys swing capably from tree to tree. Many of our neighbouring tribes eat monkeys, but we do not. They are sacred to our religion.

It is a sin to kill a monkey.

***

The sun beats down on us as we continue our journey towards the river. My uncle continues to tell me tales of the white people. In the middle of a story, my father waves his hand, and my uncle falls silently. My heart races as I take in my surroundings, so different to the jungle that I know.

Pale skinned men are running around huge… contraptions? I do not know what they are. They are red and yellow, and shiny, and huge, but foreign to me. The men are shouting at each other in a strange language and they laugh. Trees are lying on the floor, splintered, burned, and monkeys lie on the ground next to them. Monkeys, lizards, birds. I let out a whimper and my father hushes me. When I can bring myself to look again there is a lonely leopard wandering towards the pack of men. She is prowling, her coat glistening in the harsh sunlight.

The men spot her and appear frightened for a moment. One takes out one of those metal weapons that my uncle told me about. He aims it at her and there's a loud bang that makes me jump out of my skin. It echoes off the remaining trees as the leopard falls to the ground. The men laugh again and walk towards her, using ropes to tie her up. They kick her, prod her with a stick, throw stones at her.

Tears are flowing easily from my eyes now. How could they be doing this? Do they not have hearts? They could have just scared her away, but they are torturing her. She struggles against the ropes they have put around her, but the men just laugh and continue their disgraceful games. My father is angry. Very angry. He picks up his bow, puts an arrow in it, aims it at one of the foreigners. My uncle tries to stop him, tugging at his shoulders. I try too, for killing him will not make things any better. I

'Leopard' by Morgan Joy Ashby

know the others will come after us, find our family. They are cruel. They are twisted. Killing them will only make things worse. I try to tell my father that, but he releases the arrow before we have a chance to stop him.

As we run my uncle continues to tell me stories about the men, attempting to make me forget the seriousness of our situation. He tells me they capture the beautiful creatures of the jungle. They put them in big vehicles and take them far away, to cold parts of the world. They lock them up in cages and feed them pieces of raw meat. Children come to see them, prod things through the bars of their cages, whisper silly things to the animals.

He calls these places "Zoos". The word is not in the language that we know, and we have no word for a place like that. Animals don't belong there. Animals belong out here with us. Free.

About the author

This story was written by Kristen-Anne Bowen, who lives in Pembrokeshire, Wales with her family and her dog, Jet. She likes writing because it takes her to whole new worlds where she can be whoever she wants to be, wherever she wants to be, whenever she wants to be, and she loves feeling that freedom.
It means a lot to Kristen-Anne to be published in this book as she has been writing from a young age and has always wanted to be published and become an author. Her favourite books are *Angel Cake* and *Cherry Crush*, both by Cathy Cassidy, *New Moon* by Stephanie Meyer and the *His Dark Materials* trilogy by Philip Pullman.

This short story is inspired by and dedicated to all animals in captivity – who deserve to be free.

The Paws Writing Competition
Your chance to be published

Thank you for reading this very special book and we hope you enjoyed it and that it brings you a little closer to understanding the emotions of wild animals. All the children I think have really captured this. It is amazing how varied the stories are.

If, like the children that entered the Paws Competition, you are also a child that loves to write or you're the parent or teacher of a child that does, then why not enter the competition yourself or encourage your child to.

We hope to run the Paws Writing Competition regularly and the 2012 competition will run from **September until the end of January 2013**. Do tell your schools and friends and why not sign up for the Paws Newsletter on our website so you don't miss out. Also look out for free giveaways of our animal books!

www.pawsnclawspublishing.co.uk

You can download posters about the next writing competition, with all the information for your schools, libraries, groups you might belong to… later this year.

You never know, your story might be in the next *Wild n Free* book!

PAWS FOR THOUGHT

Teachers and Parents

The questions in this book – further discussion

Throughout the book I have included questions, suggested that children might like to find out more about some of the animals they have read about, perhaps have a discussion about it in class. I've talked about animals you might never have heard of, like the Fossa, or the Nepalese Wild Cat. I've spoken about the effect that alien species can have on native populations, like the Grey Squirrel, suggested you might discuss this. I have talked about nature in all its wonderful guises, like the brood parasite, and how some species breed with other closely related ones to form hybrids, like the zorse. I have also talked about evolution, conservation and animal protection from practices like the ivory trade and what we might do, however small to reduce the effects of Global Warming.

Many of the children have written about poachers, and a common theme has been how Man has been an enemy and how his practices have impacted on animals. Of course we also know that many humans do care and do show great kindness to animals.

We hope some of the questions and other questions that arise while reading this book, will lead to further discussion. And we really hope children will want to know more about the animals they've read about and do some of their own research, maybe even write their own story. We would love for schools/groups to really embrace some of the questions raised in this book.

If you would like to take that a step further and take part in a PAWS workshop then do check out our website and talk to your schools. Does your school have trips to the zoo? Have you thought about the animals in zoos and wildlife parks? Are they really there to make money or do they really put a lot of money into conservation? With the majority of zoos it's so much smaller than you might think.

Do you think we should have zoos? Perhaps you might even encourage your school to have an alternative to the zoo trip? Perhaps you would like to attend one of these workshops instead?

**To find out more about PAWS visit the
Paws n Claws website:**

*www.pawsnclawspublishing.co.uk/Pages/
PAWSWorkshopScheme.aspx*

Other opportunities at Paws n Claws

**Calling Budding Young Reporters… 16 or under
Fancy writing us a report about a wild animal?**

**You can write anything up to about 500 words, it
needs to be factual and educational and it has to be
about a WILD ANIMAL.**

Choose a wild animal, tell us some facts about it, where
it lives, what it eats, what are the biggest dangers it faces?
How many are left in the wild and what can we do to
help it? There are a lot of links and information on the
Born Free Website but you can use books… make sure
the information is accurate! Why not look in the local
library?

Our favourites each month will be here on the website
and you'll get a special certificate to say you're our
Wildlife Reporter of the Month.

Remember to tell your school friends and teachers…
you might all want to have a go… even work on
something together.

Read about this on our website
www.pawsnclawspublishing.co.uk

Index

*(Page numbers in **bold type** refer to illustrations)*

Other books by Paws n Claws that help wild animals

Paws n Claws Publishing specialises in fictional books about animals and every book makes a donation to the Born Free Foundation.

To find out more about us visit our website:
www.pawsnclawspublishing.co.uk

To find out more about The Jet-Set and to sign up for our fun animal newsletter visit: *www.thejet-set.com*

If you want to learn about the Born Free Foundation and their children's Wild Crew Club visit:
http://www.bornfree.org.uk/kids-go-wild/wildcrew/

Other books you might enjoy...

Hipp-O-Dee-Doo-Dah
For children

You'll find all sorts of animals in this collection of stories – a hippo who longs for water, a chimp that proves to be tougher than a gorilla, a horse only two people can see, a cat that cooks, a starfish that falls from the sky and dogs that save lives.

There are some amazing people too – the young girl who looks after her mum, some young people who have magical powers they have to hide, a boy who finds a new way to remember his grandfather, and a young man who has the universe at his command but daren't let others see.

All of the stories are about how people are thoughtful with each other or with the animals in their care. And they'll bring sunshine to a grey day.

Hipp-O-Dee-Doo-Dah features stories by Blue Peter Award winners Lauren St John and Alan Gibbons, and a foreword by Michael Morpurgo OBE.

£1 from the sale of each copy, plus a percentage of the author royalties, will be donated to Children's Hospices UK (now Together for Short Lives).

ISBN 978-1-907335-11-2

Order from Amazon, bookshops or *www.bridgehousepublishing*.co.uk

Gentle Footprints
Edited by Debz Hobbs-Wyatt

Animal Short Stories (but written for adults so this book contains some adult language)

Gentle Footprints is a wonderful collection of short stories about wild animals. The stories are fictional but each story gives a real sense of the wildness of the animal, true to the Born Free edict that animals should be born free and should live free. The animals range from the octopus to the elephant, each story beautifully written. Gentle Footprints includes a new and highly original story by Richard Adams, author of *Watership Down*, and a foreword by the patron of Born Free, Virginia McKenna OBE.

£1 from the sale of each copy, plus a percentage of the author royalties, will be donated to The Born Free Foundation.

As featured on Mariella Frostrup's Book Show at Hay, 2010 and on ITV's Loose Women.

ISBN 978-1-907335-04-4

Order from Amazon, bookshops or *www.bridgehousepublishing.co.uk*

Lightning Source UK Ltd.
Milton Keynes UK
UKOW051032200612

194726UK00001B/14/P